"STERLING NOEL . . . has mastered the art of suspense writing as few others have been able to do."
—*Springfield (Mo.) News & Leader*

You will agree with this laudatory comment when you read Sterling Noel's latest spy-thriller, *Run For Your Life*, a fast-paced, tensely exciting novel of international intrigue, which we are proud to present as AN AVON ORIGINAL.

Here is what the critics have said about Noel's previous books:

"Top-notch . . . not a dull, dragging line in it."
—*Montgomery Advertiser*

"Hard-hitting, hard-kissing, suspenseful."
—*New York Times*

"Packed with vigorous action."
—*Pittsburgh Press*

"Fast-moving . . . exploits the elements of suspense to the limit."
—*Ft. Lauderdale News*

Run

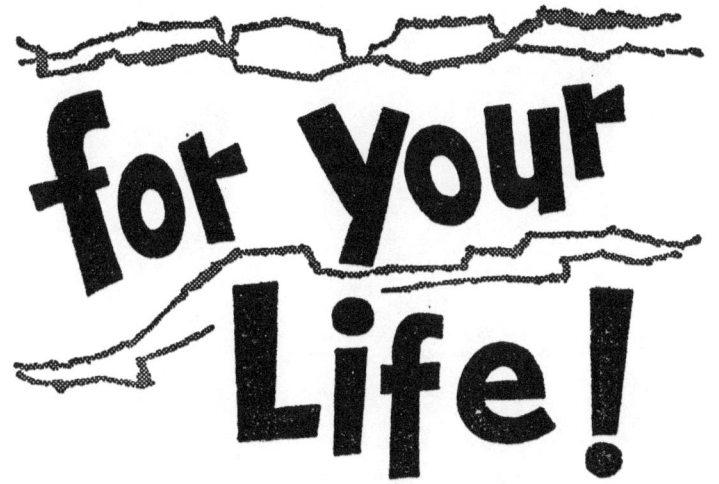

for your Life!

STERLING NOEL

WILDSIDE PRESS

1

THE MAN STOOD on the small balcony looking down. He was of medium height and broad of shoulder—the build of one physically active, proud of his body and of himself. His tweed suit had been recently pressed and was spotless. Only the knot of his tie, which had been pulled to one side of his collar, betrayed any of the struggle that had preceded his appearance on the balcony.

If one had been able to see his face close up, he would have marked the wooden set of the features and eyes that stared unseeing, in the manner of a sightless person. It was as though he had been drugged.

His body was inclined forward, his thighs pressing against the low railing of the balcony. The glass of the French door behind him to his left reflected the setting sun. This door was open a few inches and in the room behind it there were shadows moving so that you knew he was not alone.

He stood there for a few minutes—less than five. Then suddenly his body jack-knifed forward and plunged downward.

The balcony remained empty. No one came out of the room to see what had happened to the man. The shadows within vanished. The single thud from the cobbles five stories below echoed in the empty afternoon.

2

THERE WAS A RESPECTABLE, well-regarded gent by the name of Randall McCarey who counted the money and locked up the safe every night in the National Bank of

Eastmoreland, Virginia, which once had belonged to his maternal grandfather, and who firmly believed that he had found peace and an acceptable life in a community of his own. He considered himself to be well adjusted and, although not ecstatically happy, at least satisfied enough most of the time with his activities and his friends. He would have been much surprised indeed if anyone had questioned his way of life or his attitude towards it. I know all about this man and his thoughts and his beliefs because I am Randall McCarey of Eastmoreland, Virginia.

That is the calm, untroubled way it was until a certain day in a small resort town in southern France on the Côte d'Azur, where this Randall McCarey shouldn't have been anyway. That's one place you could begin this story of de Lys and Barodi and de Castro and Vico del Oro and the women Martita and Suzanne, among the many others. But also, and just as logically, you could go back some eight years, when I first assumed the name of McCarey, or back even twenty years when de Castro signed the manifests and receipts for the Spanish Republican Government. But let's start with Eastmoreland on April 17, 1956, when a tall, graying man known to me as Colonel John Updyke came a-calling at the bank. I'll tell you about what went before as it is needed to make this history hang together.

This April 17 dawned much like the other days of that spring in the Northern Neck—cool with the promise of sun and the land coming back to life. I bathed and shaved as usual in the bathroom that Dottie and I had once shared. It was a big bathroom that she had designed and the sunken tub could have held a whole family. I used my own washbasin, which was the one on the left, and I thought about her as I always did in the mornings, but not with any overwhelming sadness. Dottie had been gone for three years and I was used to being without her. I had even stopped visiting her grave. Maybe I'm not the constant or sentimental type. Maybe I forget.

Marie had my usual breakfast of bacon and eggs, toast and coffee waiting when I was dressed and went to the sun porch. She made her comments on the weather, the local school board, the President, as usual and in that

6

order, then vanished into her kitchen. Just another day. An ordinary day, with luncheon at twelve-thirty with Old Lawson, then bridge in the evening with the Howells or the Gideons or the Carters, and with Nancy or Sue-Anne or Lucy-Jo, who were known locally as the aching women, to make a fourth. I had no objection to them so long as they didn't ache for me. I was over that sort of thing. So I thought.

I let myself into the bank with my own key at nine a.m., spoke a greeting to the porter and the guard, then went to my desk and started sorting out the day's business. The tellers, clerks, and sundry others would arrive by nine-thirty and Old Lawson would make his formal entrance at ten o'clock on the dot. It had always been that way. It would always be that way so long as Lawson held up and until I moved into his chair. Why change it?

It was nine-fourteen, give or take a few seconds, that a minor change set in, however. This was heralded by a sharp rapping on the front door and the ensuing remonstrance by Harry the guard with a stranger who sought admittance. Apparently this early caller satisfied Harry quickly, for he was brought to my desk. He was tall and stooped and gray and he had the rugged features of a second-rate movie heavy. He smiled at me, held out a hand and said, "Alex, you're looking fit."

I got up from my chair and shook his hand. This was Colonel John Updyke of Bureau-X. He had never been a friend of mine, although we had once worked closely on a vicious, murderous affair in and around Algiers. I said:

"It's good to see you again, Colonel, but the name isn't Alex. It's Randall McCarey. Don't tell me your memory is getting short."

He kept his smile and shook his head. "Alex is good enough," he replied. "We've got a job for you."

It was my turn to shake my head. "I've got a job. Just say good-bye, Colonel, and leave quietly."

He laughed then. "You're still the same fresh bastard you always were. Mind if I sit down?"

He sat in the customer's chair. I felt nothing particularly. I was safe in my bank and the hell with Bureau-X and all of its works. That was for adolescents anyway.

7

"Do you remember Provence in 1942?" he asked, lighting a cigarette with my desk lighter. "You were dropped from a plane at Frejus and you waited for a couple of days until the Germans quieted down, then you hot-footed it to Grasse to see a man in the *maquis* by the name of Arbori."

I nodded. "Julo Arbori," I said. "A stinker."

"Yes, a rat, but helpful to us nevertheless for a time—until his demise. Well, there was another man associated with him during that period and we have reason to believe that you knew him, or at least met him. In fact, it now develops that you are the only one whom we know of who might have known this other man and his background."

"What about him?" I asked.

"We need him identified."

"Well, bring him around. Banking hours are from ten a.m. to two-thirty p.m., and I am here every day except Saturdays, Sundays and the usual holidays."

He crushed out his cigarette in my Carol Stupel ashtray and gave me a hard look. "I am not in the humor for clowning," he admonished. "This is very serious business for us."

"Go soak your head," I said mildly. "I'm not interested in you or your serious business. I've been trying to tell you that in a nice way. If you want me to make my point differently, I'll be happy to oblige you. I'm still big enough to throw you out of this bank. Do I make myself clear?"

He sat back in his chair then and smiled. "I know I have always antagonized you. I wish it were not that way. We need your help desperately. It will mean a trip to Europe, all expenses paid. We will not require your services for more than a week. Perhaps less. Can't we arrange this in a friendly manner?"

"I don't see how," I replied.

"Would it mean anything to you that Pete Dumbrowsky is seriously involved?"

"Why should it? He's drawing his salary."

"My guess is that he won't be drawing his salary for long unless we can move quickly, and we can't move at all without any identification."

"You spy-chasers getting legal?"

8

"It's not a question of legality. If we get the wrong man we get nothing."

I thought about Pete, the Detroit Pole with the intuition of a Hecate, who had saved my skin at Belgrade in 1941. I remembered his infectious good humor and his unquestioning loyalty. I thought about that Belgrade caper some more, then I said, "One week and all expenses. Where do I go?"

He nodded as though he had expected my answer. "The Côte d'Azur. We'll fly you to Paris by commercial airline and then to Nice in one of our own planes. We'll have a car there for you and a rendezvous. It'll be in the Frejus area—most likely at St. Raphael. You will meet Dumbrowsky. He will ask you to look at his man and tell us who he is."

"Suppose I don't know?"

He shrugged. "Suppose you don't? We lose. But at least we'll be able to cover Pete. We can't go near him until we try for this identification."

"Pete can take care of himself," I said.

Updyke nodded. "He used to be able to. We're all a bit older now, you know."

I didn't feel any older and I looked my skepticism. "It's still the same racket. Pete'll make out. But now for the ninety-seven cent question: Who do you think this mystery man may be?"

Updyke settled back for a long dissertation. He reached back into a score of years gone and came up with the Spanish Civil War. He named a dozen "freedom" fighters and he waited for me to react. I didn't. None of the names had any meaning to me. Then he switched to Hitler's invasion of the Balkan countries and he named more names. Three of them I had heard before—but my memory was rusty and the lessons of Deschines and Baker and others had slipped away. I didn't know how to remember now, beyond the daily requirements of the banking business.

"I've heard three of those names," I said.

"How about Sandor Barodi? Is that one of them?"

"Yes . . . but it wasn't at that time. Barodi was later."

"How much later? The War?"

"I think it was the War."

"Not in Grasse, in 1942?"

9

"Perhaps. It could have been in Grasse."

"With Arbori?"

"Probably. I'd say it was with Arbori."

"Then you'd know him again if you saw him?"

"I don't connect any face with the name. I'd have to have a look at him."

The Colonel got to his feet. "Can you come with me now?"

I looked at the clock over the vault door. Nine fifty-eight. "Give me about seven minutes," I said. "I've got to tell the old man."

3

I BOARDED a plane at Idlewild at six-thirty that evening and I disembarked the next day at noon at Orly, ahead of schedule because of a strong tail-wind. A short, square Frenchman who mumbled a name that sounded like Barsac as he pumped my hand, took my small bag and led me to a black Citroën that was parked on the apron and helped me into the back seat. A mustachioed ancient behind the wheel gave me a toothless grin, then took off like the start of the Grand Prix, scattering the ground crew that was taking over my plane. He drove with heedless *vitesse* across the south side of the field, over runways, gravel and grass, to a hangar bearing the name of an oil company. He skidded to a stop by the hangar door, turned to give me another of his grins, then pulled his cap down over his eyes and settled down to doze.

I climbed out of the car and looked around. Nobody. I walked into the hangar and looked over two French Mystères parked inside. I'd never seen one up close, although I'd read their specifications years before. I'd been checked out in our own Sabres before I left Bureau-X and so I was interested. I didn't see the man until he was almost beside me.

He was tall, thin, and unfriendly. He asked me in angry

10

French what the hell I thought I was doing in this hangar here. I said I was waiting for an airplane. He scowled at that, then motioned me outside. "Outside," he said.

Something came over me. Insanity, probably. I wasn't a banker any more, but this knucklehead from Bureau-X used to knock 'em over with one blow from his mighty fist. I swung this mighty fist of the former Alexis Bodine, then, but it must have turned into a powder puff. I got up from the concrete slowly and painfully and rubbed my jaw. I said in my rusty French, "What's the idea, huh?"—or words to that effect. The tall, thin type sneered at me and motioned once more with his hand. "Outside," he said. "Like I told you."

At that unhappy juncture the aged pilot of the Citroën came into the hangar, grinning his toothless grin. He told his countryman: "You will go up to the *bureau*, you species of cow, and you will fetch M. Lagrange, and you will apologize to the monsieur here for being a species of cow, is it not so?"

The thin one glared at the ancient chauffeur but did as he was told. He apologized to me reluctantly, then was off and up a stairway in the rear, which I hadn't seen before. The chauffeur put a friendly hand on my shoulder. "That was foolish," he said. "At your age—tut tut."

I didn't have any answer for that. I brushed off my clothes and refrained from defending my age. I suppose I was learning to curb that impulse.

M. Lagrange was devastated. He had not expected me for an hour. Would I come with him and join him in an aperitif or a cup of tea? My, what a vicious person was that Henri, but of course one needed such people about, things being as they were in the world, was it not so? It went on that way as we walked to the back of the hangar and up the stairway to the offices. Then he said as I sat in a chair beside his desk, "You are very well known to some of us in France. I am told you are the one who killed Arbori."

"That story got out just after the war," I replied. "No, I can't say that I killed Arbori. We didn't like him but we found him useful."

"You deny it, then?" he asked.

11

Henri brought a tray with tea for me and a *vermout cassis* for Lagrange.

"No," I said, "I can't deny it. It's just that I can't *say* I killed Arbori. Actually I don't know. I may have killed him. I think not, but I may have."

"Who else may have killed him?" he asked.

I shook my head. "It was a general melee. A lot of people."

"I think you did it from what I hear. You should not have come back to France. I am telling you that for your own good, monsieur. For my part, I admire you. To me, you deserve high honors from my country. But Arbori had many friends and relatives and they have not forgotten. No, you should not have come back to France."

I was flown to Nice in one of the Mystères. The cockpit had been rigged for training and there was room for two side by side, packed close. The pilot was an uncommunicative young Niceoise who showed an irritating deference to my age. He assured me he would go not too fast and not too high up.

"Hell," I said, "I was flying these things before you were out of kindergarten."

"Many men of your age tell me that," he said.

It was a lousy trip.

I was met at the Nice airport by a dame in a trench coat who was too fat around the hips. Let me make myself clear. I am not generally critical of women who overeat. But this one was *much* too fat. She knew me immediately. She called me by name—that is, the name I had discarded so many years before—Alex Bodine. She spoke like an American from the Middle West, although there were overtones of a sojourn in London. She escorted me to a black Simca which was too small for her *derrière* and she told me she would drive me as far as Cannes, then would give me the car and I would be on my own. She gave me an international driver's license made out in the name of Randall McCarey, to match my passport, and the papers for the car, also made out to me.

12

"Haven't I seen you before?" I asked as I settled beside her and she took off.

"No. But I am Eleanor's sister."

"Not Fat Eleanor of Washington Street?"

"Yes. I'm Fat Mildred."

"I'm sorry."

"Don't be. I know I eat too much. I do it all by myself."

I looked down at my own banker's pot. "So do I."

"You're not what I expected at all," she said. "Eleanor told me all about you years ago—you and Dottie."

"Yeah. I'm not the same man." I was thinking of the incident at the Orly hangar. "But I'm not in this espionage business any more either, so I suppose it doesn't make much difference."

"It makes a difference—to both of us. We tell ourselves that it doesn't, but it does. We meet up with some disappointment that we can't handle and we let ourselves go. We get sloppy all over and we don't care how we look or what becomes of us. . . . Your wife died, didn't she?"

"Yes, Dottie died. It was an automobile accident—or it was made to look like an automobile accident."

"You just let it go at that?"

"No, I fussed around for about a year, but Bureau-X wouldn't give me any help and neither would anyone else. Duganov was dead, so I didn't have any leads. Besides, I was working in a bank, trying to make a life for myself."

"I guess you just deteriorated."

"What do you mean by that?"

"You used to be hell on wheels. There wasn't anyone who could go up against you. I heard about you."

"Yesterday at Orly a tall, thin guy about thirty knocked me down with his fist."

"Well, don't hang around these precincts, that's all. There are too many people hereabouts with long memories who don't like you. . . . They tell me you killed Arbori."

"Arbori again! God damn it, suppose I did kill Arbori! What of it?"

"Yank, go home."

"O.K., Mildred, I'll go home. But stop pushing me."

She laughed. "Even Fat Mildred can push Alex Bodine these days."

13

"Nuts."

She drove to the Martinez Hotel in Cannes and got out. She said: "You go on to St. Raphael. Register at the Hotel Beau Sejour, down on the beach. Someone will get in touch with you. Good-bye, Alex."

I shook her hand. "Good-bye, Mildred. Thanks for the ride and the car."

She waved a hand at me and walked into the hotel. I slid into the driver's seat and took off. It was two o'clock and I'd had no lunch. I decided I'd go to the Voile au Vent and induce them to fix me some *poulet estragon*. Then I looked at my stomach and I stopped at a bistro instead and had coffee and one *croissant*. I took the Corniche de l'Esterel and drove at my leisure, admiring the Med on the one hand, the villas of the rich on the other. Outside of Le Trayas there was a huge stone pile that looked at least like the summer palace of an emperor—that is in the days when emperors were holding. It must have had eighty rooms and there were a hundred fancy cars parked in front of it. A house party, undoubtedly.

As I approached the main driveway of the villa an open Jaguar roared down and fishtailed into the highway, causing me to jam on my brakes and skid my wheels. There were a couple of dames in the Jag, their heads bare and their hair flying. One was a gorgeous redhead, driving, and the other was a gorgeous blonde. The redhead waved at me and made a gesture with her hand that might have been obscene, in the manner of the Italians. It made me feel good. I was living again. I'd just gotten what might have been a dirty gesture from a redheaded doll with enough allure to be invited to an emperor's castle. I squared my shoulders and drove a little faster.

I got into St. Raphael about four and checked into the Beau Sejour. There was a reservation for me but it would not have been needed. There were less than a dozen guests at the hotel so early in the season. The Riviera can be a cold place in the spring.

I got a double room overlooking the *plage* and unpacked my one small handbag which contained a razor and other toilet articles, a couple of shirts that you washed and hung up wet and that needed no ironing, and socks and under-

14

wear of similar material. I had learned to travel light away back with Bureau-X and it was a strong habit. Even a handbag was a luxury. In those days I seldom had carried more than would fit into my pockets.

I sat down to wait. I read *Le Matin*, a copy of which went with the room. I dozed, I listened to the London Symphony playing Ravel, broadcast from Marseilles, then I dozed again. One circuit of the hour hand and I said to hell with it. I put on my coat and went down to the bar. There were two sad *poules* at one end perched on stools and talking to the barkeep. They brightened considerably when I came in and one, a small, plump, dark girl with too much lipstick on her too-wide mouth, gave me a long, appraising look. The other, who had stringy blonde hair and pimples, raised her voice a couple of decibles and allowed as how she would have another *coupe*. Then she tossed me what was supposed to be a sly smile, which was to indicate that I could pay for it if I chose.

I didn't choose. I sat at the other end of the bar and asked for a double Scotch and soda. I turned my back on them and sipped it, looking out the window to the deserted street and the promenade beyond that rimmed the beach. There is a deep sadness about a resort out of season. Without the warmth of the summer sun and the gaily attired people crowding together to enjoy themselves, you have nothing but bleak emptiness and peeling paint. You have the memories of last season and the season before, but you have no present. Today is waiting for tomorrow's revival. You wait, that's all—just as the two *poules* and the bartender were waiting. You have nothing else to do until the season bursts forth with its throng.

A newsboy came in and left a paper with the bartender. Then he came up to me and asked me if I would have a *Paris-Soir*. I shook my head. He touched a grimy finger to my shoulder and said in an urgent whisper, "You should have a *Paris-Soir*, monsieur. You should."

I turned towards him and saw two earnest eyes in a swarthy face much too old for the rest of him. He couldn't have been more than fifteen, yet his face was that of an old man. He grinned at me and his teeth were brown and uneven.

"Why should I have a *Paris-Soir*?" I asked.

He put a paper in my lap and whispered, "Turn to the first inside page." Then he was gone, scooting out of the door into the street.

I put my drink down on the bar and picked up the paper. The two *poules* and the bartender were looking at me. When I glanced up at them they averted their eyes and joined again in their conversation. I opened the paper to the first inside page. Written across the top of it in pencil was the note: *"Allez au cour Nouvel Hotel. Vite."*—"Go to courtyard Nouvel Hotel. Hurry."

I folded the paper and called the bartender. I paid him for the Scotch and asked him where the Hotel Nouvel found itself. He told me to walk east to the next corner, turn left, and proceed to the middle of the second block. "There it rests," he said.

I left the Beau Sejour bar and found the air had grown cooler with the approach of evening. I needed a topcoat but I didn't have one. I hurried east on the boulevard Liberation to the corner, then turned left on the rue Honoré-Vadon and strode the short distance to the Nouvel. It was a small hostelry with a restaurant on the street floor and containing not more than a dozen rooms. The restaurant was dark at this early hour. I could see inside the hall where there was a desk and a dim light shining above it. There was no one in sight. I paused just an instant, then continued on to large double doors beyond the building which would open onto the courtyard. Parked opposite the doors was a closed, box-like vehicle painted a dull black. On the side panel was a faded red cross and under it the barely legible word, "Ambulance."

I tried one of the double doors and it opened. I stepped inside under an arch and strolled past the concierge's lodge. Over to the left of the cobbled courtyard, near the hotel wall, was a group of five men. Two were kneeling and looking at an object on the ground. The *gendarmes* stood a little off, also looking down. A man in a white coat was facing the *gendarmes* and lighting a cigarette. As I approached, all five faces turned towards me. All action seemed to suspend, waiting for my arrival.

I stopped before the *gendarmes* and dug deep for plaus-

16

ible words. "I was to meet someone," I said. "Is there anything wrong?"

One of the men who had been kneeling rose to his feet and stepped to my side. "Whom were you to meet?" he asked.

I shrugged. "A friend. An old friend."

He took my arm in a vice-like grip and turned me toward the object on the ground. He pointed his finger dramatically. "You were to meet him?" he asked.

I looked down at a body. It was that of a man in a tweed suit, recently pressed. The knot of his tie was askew and one leg was bent grotesquely under his hip. He was lying on his side and I could not see his face clearly from that angle. The man who held my arm led me around to a better vantage point. I leaned closer to make certain.

It was Pete Dumbrowsky.

4

THE NEAREST *sous-préfecture* to St. Raphael is at Grasse, and so I found myself once more in this center of perfumes and *maquis* intrigue—when there was a *maquis*. I was taken thither by Inspector Jordain and his associate, Sergeant Hesse, who had been the two bending over the inert remains of my friend Dumbrowsky when I entered the courtyard. Sergeant Hesse drove the police Renault and Jordain kept me company in the back seat. En route they plied me with questions interspersed with their own speculation.

As we neared Cannes the Inspector asked me for the dozenth time why this man Dumbrowsky should have leaped to his death just before he had had an appointment with me.

"It is not logical," the Inspector said. "Here you have come all the way from America so that you can spend your vacation with him—or so you say—and he does not have the decency to stay alive to greet you."

"It is not altogether a matter of decency," I protested. "Perhaps he was troubled."

"It was a woman," said Sergeant Hesse. "I am certain it was a woman."

"What was a woman?" demanded the Inspector.

"That drove him to take his life," said the Sergeant. "One always hunts for the woman in such cases."

"Bah!" exclaimed the Inspector. "There was no proper evidence of a woman having been in his room. You yourself remarked upon that."

"But there was *some* evidence," insisted the Sergeant. "Just because the bed was not mussed. . . . There were the flecks of face powder in the bathroom and the faint trace of lipstick on the towel. I remember the case of the farmer Grissom who was supposed to have shot himself with his own gun at Cogolin, and all the time it was the fat little housemaid from Grimaud whom he had gotten with child."

"That was different."

"It was a suicide and yet it was a murder, and the woman did it."

"Monsieur Dumbrowsky was not shot and he was not murdered."

"Perhaps he was pushed. Have you thought of that, monsieur Inspector?"

"I have thought of it. What good does it do to think of it?" He turned back to me. "What woman did this monsieur associate with?"

I shook my head. "I've explained, Inspector, that I have not seen him for many years and that I know nothing of his recent life. He mentioned no women in any of his letters to me."

"Ah! Letters! Have you any of these letters, monsieur?"

"No. I did not keep them. There was nothing of significance in any of them."

"You could not possibly judge that," said the Sergeant. "Perhaps he mentioned a woman. . . ."

"I have said not," I reminded him.

"You could be mistaken, monsieur."

"That is not the question," said the Inspector. "What we want to know is, why did this monsieur take his life?"

After we had negotiated the traffic of Cannes and were

on the highway to Grasse, the Inspector took it up again. "It is very odd, monsieur, that you should have come to the courtyard just in time to find the body of your friend. Why did you come to the courtyard just then?"

It was a good question. I wished I had a good answer. "It seems to me, if you will permit me to make a suggestion, that one should inquire into M. Dumbrowsky's financial situation. As you know, I am a banker, and he often wrote to me of his investments in France. I think we may find an answer to your question there, Inspector."

"You do? Now that is an excellent suggestion, monsieur. Excellent. Sergeant, make a note of that."

"You forget I am driving."

"Well, make a note of it when we get to Grasse then." He turned back to me and sighed. "One never has enough assistance on such cases. I don't know how we can be expected to be everywhere at once. It is by the merest accident that we were in St. Raphael in the first place, and the good Lord knows what would have happened if we had left it up to the local police. . . . Tell me, monsieur, why did you come to the courtyard just at that time?"

"I was passing, on my way into the hotel to meet my friend. I looked in the courtyard and there you all were. I was curious, nothing more."

"Well, of course. I can understand that."

"But the door was closed," said the Sergeant.

"Oh yes, but I closed it," I said.

"You did?" asked the Inspector.

"It was closed before he came in," said the Sergeant.

"How could I have seen you in the courtyard if the door was closed?" I demanded.

"That is an excellent point," said the Inspector. "I quite agree. You could not have seen us if the door had been closed."

"He opened it," said the Sergeant.

"Opened it!" I exclaimed. "With what? I do not have a key! You may search me and you will find no key."

"Then the concierge opened it."

"Very likely," I said with scorn. "If I had rung you would have heard the bell, would you not?"

"An excellent point," said the Inspector.

"Nevertheless the door was closed," said the Sergeant.

"It is your word against mine," I said. "I'll tell you what we will do, Sergeant, we will toss a coin for it. If it is heads, then you are right. If the obverse, then you shall concede that the door was open."

"A good way to settle it," agreed the Inspector. He produced a one-hundred-franc piece from his pocket and handed it to me. "Here, toss this."

I tossed it. I caught it and opened my palm in front of the Inspector. The Sergeant had slowed down the car and turned back to look. It came up heads.

"There, heads! You were right, Sergeant," I said.

He nodded his head, satisfied, and turned back to his driving. "I knew it," he said. "The door was closed."

"I'm glad we got that point settled," said the Inspector. . . . "Well, here we are in Grasse. Just a few questions by the Chief Inspector so that we shall all be satisfied with this unfortunate affair and we shall take you back to St. Raphael. We are sorry to trouble you, monsieur."

It proved to be not difficult to satisfy the officials at the *sous-préfecture* that I had no connection with the death of Pete Dumbrowsky. I sat in a large room with the Chief Inspector, several aides, including Jordain and Hesse, and a stenographer. I answered all of the questions that were asked, the stenographer made notes, and then we waited until the notes were typed so that I could sign them. Off in a corner and taking no part in the proceedings was a suave, city-type policeman. He sat in a chair tilted against a wall and chain-smoked brown paper cigarettes. His eyes were closed most of the time and he had a bored, old-world expression on his face. Jordain whispered to me that this was Pierre Delacroix of the *Sûreté Générale*. "He is everywhere," he said. "He misses nothing."

After I signed the transcript I shook hands with the Chief Inspector and his aides and assured them that it had been no trouble. Inspector Jordain and Sergeant Hesse were in a hurry to get back to St. Raphael. We strolled together to the main hall of the prefecture and we were joined there by the *Sûreté* man, who came up to Jordain and put a hand on his shoulder.

"How are you, Inspector?" he said, and he nodded to me.

"This is M. Delacroix," said Jordain, introducing me.

I shook hands with him and he said, "I should like to speak with you, if you have the time. Would you join me in an *apértif*?"

"We were just returning M. McCarey to St. Raphael," said Jordain. "I must be back there before dinnertime."

"I'll run him back," said Delacroix. "I've got to be passing that way this evening."

It was agreed, then, and Jordain and the Sergeant bade me adieu. Delacroix told me he would take me to the only café in Grasse that amounted to anything, and we walked to the Bianchi on the cours Honoré Cresp. On the way he talked amiably, telling me a little about himself. He said he had been born in Provence but raised and educated in Paris. "I like my home country," he said. "Much of it is bleak and many of the farms are not productive, but the sun makes up for all of that."

At the Bianchi we sat on a small terrace and ordered vermouth. It was a restaurant I had known well in 1942 and the years following, when Grasse had been the headquarters for our *maquis* operations. I was not surprised to see old Jules Simon come to wait upon us. He was not much changed by the passing years—just a little more ancient, a few more wrinkles in his ugly face, and his hand a little less steady. All through those troubled years he had been a *maquis* stalwart and had never deviated from our resolve to drive the Germans out of France, as had so many others. . . . He gave me not a glance as he came to our table. My face had been altered some by Bureau-X for my Russian sortie, and perhaps I looked to him not at all like the Alex Bodine who had once been his friend.

When he came with our drinks he said, "Your voice is familiar, monsieur."

"I have never been here before," I replied.

He looked at me with watery, red eyes and nodded. "It is just as monsieur says." Then he shuffled away.

Delacroix said, "But as a matter of fact, monsieur has been here before, is it not so?"

I smiled at him. "No, I was on the Riviera before the War, but never in Grasse."

"And your name is Randall McCarey?"

"That's right."

"But you were a friend of this Peter Dumbrowsky, nevertheless?"

"Right."

"Did you ever hear of a man known as Alexis Bodine?"

"Yes, I've heard of him."

"He was a friend of M. Dumbrowsky also?"

"I believe he was."

"What has happened to M. Bodine?"

"He is probably still about and nothing has happened to him."

"You are wrong," said Delacroix. "He is not still about —unless. . . ."

I let the unasked question sit where it was. "You wanted to talk to me," I said. "Was this the subject?"

He looked at me out of steady blue eyes, a policeman look that was calculated to instill terror in the hearts of liars. "The Sûreté had good sources of information," he said. "We would like you to leave France, M. McCarey. We will take no formal action at this time, but we would like you to depart. Do I make myself clear?"

"No," I said, "you do not. I will have to have a reason."

"You know the reason."

"That is quibbling."

He got angry, then, and he squinted his eyes at me. "Whoever you are, you have no official standing," he said, cutting each word off short. "We will give you twenty-four hours to get out of our country."

I told him to go soak his head, using an expressive French idiom that one does not attempt to translate. His face turned red. "I will place you under detention," he said, his voice low and nasty.

"On what charge?" I asked. "Do you want to make an ass of yourself by detaining a respectable banker from our state of Virginia? . . . Come to think of it, I should go to our consulate right now and complain of the way I've been treated."

Suddenly he laughed and the tension ended. "I am no

mouse," he said, "even though I suspect you are the cat. Well, what now? Perhaps you would like to tell me something?"

I shook my head. "Nothing."

"About M. Dumbrowsky's suicide?"

"It wasn't suicide," I said. "It was a defenestration, done in the classic manner. No, my friend, it was murder, and if you know all you profess to know, then you know that."

He nodded, sipped his drink, nodded some more. "Perhaps. The *Sûreté* has no interest in M. Dumbrowsky."

"No interest in murder?"

"Don't waste your time. It will remain officially a suicide or accident. That has been decided."

"The hell it has."

5

I DON'T DEFEND any of my ensuing activities on the basis of intelligence. The intelligent thing to have done was to have gone back to Virginia and the Eastmoreland bank; to have forgotten Pete Dumbrowsky and Bureau-X and all of its works. Furthermore, I knew that this was the intelligent thing, but for a reason that eludes me completely when I try to seize upon it, I decided to go out crusading against the forces of evil and avenge Pete's death.

Put that way, it's as corny as Tennessee smoke, but underneath all of the obscure feelings that drove me on was one that I was sure of—sincerity. I believed I had to do what I was going to do; I believed that it was the only course. . . . Maybe I was bored with Virginia.

So I drove back to St. Raphael with Delacroix in his black Citroën, most of the way in silence. He had said his say to me and I never did have anything to say to him. On parting at the Hotel Beau Sejour he warned me again to leave France, adding that the *Sûreté* and the *gendarmerie* could not be responsible for my safety. This led to a fruitless discussion of safety and who's safe and who wants to be safe, in a world that's no safer than the next highway accident or the whim of a mad Slav. But he had fun with his tired old French logic and *bons mots* and I left him reasonably satisfied.

I went to my room, got my bag and checked out of the hotel. Then I went into the bar and bought a drink for one of the two *poules* still on duty—the blonde one with pimples—and the bartender. His name was Georges and hers was Yvette and she was eighteen and she came from Marseilles. This would be her second season in St. Raphael, when the season started, and it was inevitable that she was sleeping with Georges when she was not in more remunerative beds. But actually she lived with Ondine—that little dark girl she was with earlier who went home because she had a cold and there were no customers anyway— and yes, she knew the newsboy who had sold me the *Paris-Soir.*

His name was Louis and he was the natural son of the widow Gross who owned the kiosk at the railway station. Georges supplied that the Grosses lived in the building just behind the station beside the Peugeot garage on the avenue Victor Hugo.

I bade them both adieu, the *poule* and the bartender, and I went to seek Louis Gross. Always you have to start at the beginning, and Louis was the beginning of the defenestration of Pete Dumbrowsky, so far as I knew anything about it.

I found the Grosses just finished dinner in their parlor-dining room, which was much better furnished than I would have expected. Mme. Gross opened the door of the flat for me and glared at me inhospitably as I sought to explain that I wished to see her son. She was about to turn me away when the boy came to the door beside her and urged her to admit me. He told her I was a friend.

Dinner dishes were on the table and on a large platter in the center was half a *gigot.* The boy led me to a divan and turned a chair around for himself and sat facing me. Mme. Gross stood by the door, forbidding and unfriendly. She was a short, plump woman in her mid-forties and she wore a brief skirt that revealed calves as sinewy as mine.

24

She had her arms folded over forty-inch breasts and she was as sturdy as the *banque de France.*

"You wrote me a note on a newspaper," I said to him. "Who told you—"

He shook his head violently. "I did not write the note, monsieur. She did."

"She? Who?"

"The girl. She wrote it and told me to take the newspaper to the hotel and find you. She gave me five hundred francs."

"The money belongs to the boy," said Mme. Gross. "He earned it."

"Of course," I agreed. The boy was staring at me with shining jet eyes and his old-young face was as alert as a fox's. "Do you know the name of the girl?" I asked him.

He shook his head. I took out my wallet and produced a thousand-franc note, holding it towards him. "I must know her name," I said.

"Tell him," ordered Mme. Gross.

"Tita," said the boy. "I don't know her other name. She lives at No. 8 rue Honoré-Vadon."

I gave him the thousand francs and got up. Mme. Gross said, "That is hardly enough, monsieur. You have taken much of the boy's time. . . ."

"And time is money," I agreed. "But one thousand francs is enough for half a name. What is the other half?"

Mme. Gross frowned and shook her head. "I have heard it. Decassero, or some such. Yes, Decassero. That's it. Well, monsieur?"

I dipped into my wallet for another thousand francs, gave it to her and departed. I could hear them jabbering like magpies as I started down the stairs.

I went to No. 8 rue Honoré-Vadon, which was entered through the same courtyard where I had seen Pete's body, and I encountered a thin, unfriendly *concierge* who at first denied that there was anyone living in her house by the name of Tita Decassero. Two thousand francs restored the memory of her tenants and produced a pair of names that seemed more plausible. Martita de Castro was the girl's name.

"But she has gone away, monsieur," said the concierge.

"She told me she was leaving France on an extended vacation."

I brought forth two more thousand-franc notes and straightened out their dog-eared corners. "I should like to visit the mademoiselle's flat," I said. "It is most important to me that I see the view from her window so that I may determine if she is the girl who waved to me when I last stayed in the hotel."

"She waved to you?"

"Yes, madame, every morning she would greet me in such a manner. I did not have a chance to make her acquaintance because I was called away from St. Raphael suddenly."

"I can't let you visit her flat. That is out of the question."

I added two more thousand-franc notes to those in my hand and straightened their edges. The concierge looked at them for a moment, then went to the mailboxes and took a large ring of keys from a hook. She selected one, took it off the ring and laid it on the table in front of me. She reached out her hand and, with a quick gesture, took the franc notes. She said, "I cannot permit monsieur to visit Apartment 15. That is final." She turned away and went into an inner room.

I climbed four flights of dusty wood steps and knocked on the door of Apartment 15. I thought at first that I heard a sound inside, then decided I was mistaken. I inserted the key and turned it. The lock clicked but the door remained fast. I turned the key again, trying it in the other direction. The door would not budge.

It was an oak door with an opaque glass panel in the upper half. I tested the glass with my knuckles. It sounded much thicker than ordinary window glass. I took off my coat and one shoe. I held the coat against the lower corner of the glass, nearest the latch, and gave it a whack with the heel of the shoe. It cracked all right. I was examining the cracks by the light of a match when there was a voice from inside Apartment 15.

It was a feminine voice. It was low and throaty and there seemed to be a note of hysteria in it. The words were in Spanish. The voice said, "Go away or I'll shoot."

26

I replied in Spanish. I said, "I am a friend. Open the door for me." I tried it in French and English also, my Spanish being undependable.

"Go away," she said, in French and then in English. There was no doubt what she meant.

"I am the American friend of Pete Dumbrowsky," I said.

"You are lying. Go away."

"See here, you've got a gun. Open the door and have a look at me. If you don't like the way I look, then you can shoot me."

"What?"

"You can shoot me. I'll take my chances."

There were noises from inside as of a heavy object being moved. I put on my coat and my shoe. The door opened. She stood there looking at me out of deep-set china-blue eyes. In her right hand, held low and close to her body in a professional manner, was a small automatic pistol.

"I am Randall McCarey," I said. "You are Martita De Castro?"

She nodded. She looked at me out of steady eyes, making up her mind. "You might be this American," she said finally. "I will trust you just a little bit. Come in."

She backed into a small vestibule and I followed her. I closed the door behind me and noted a heavy chair that apparently had been wedged against it. She backed into a small living room, keeping the gun level all the while, and motioned for me to sit on a divan against the left wall. I sat. The room was neat, the furniture immaculate but well used. An oriental carpet had the appearance of having been scrubbed. Two candles in silver candlesticks on the sideboard were lit and there was a crucifix on the wall between them. I sat back and relaxed. I started to reach for a cigarette.

"Keep your hands in front of you," she said. "Talk. Tell me about yourself."

She stood facing me, her legs spread apart and her feet firmly planted. She was cat-like and quick. I looked at her face and into her eyes and I liked what I saw. The finely chiselled features of the well-born Spanish lady. She was about twenty-five and beautifully constructed. You might not have called her pretty, but there was too much character and personality for mere prettiness. Perhaps she was beautiful. I didn't know, just then.

"I was sent here from America to help Pete Dumbrowsky," I said. "I was at the Hotel Beau Sejour waiting to hear from him. The newsboy Louis Gross delivered a newspaper to me in the bar of the hotel. There was a note on the second page of the newspaper telling me to hurry to the courtyard of the hotel Nouvel. I went there and I saw the body of Pete, lying on the cobbles. I was questioned by the police, then taken to the *sous-préfecture* at Grasse and made to sign a statement. I returned to St. Raphael, found the newsboy, and was informed that you had written the note in the newspaper. Now I am here."

I started to reach for a cigarette again and she said, "Keep your hands still!" I smiled at her and asked, "You don't like my story?"

"It is good enough, but I have no interest in it or in you. I did merely what M. Dumbrowsky asked me to do before he died. He said to me, 'Keep a watch. If anything happens to me, send a message to M. McCarey at the Hotel Beau Sejour. Louis will carry the message.' He told me about you, yes, but that was his business and not mine."

"That's why you stay in your apartment behind locked doors, terrified, with a gun in your hand. . . ."

"Get up," she said, motioning with the gun. "You can go now."

"No," I said, "I'll stay awhile. I want to talk to you." She motioned impatiently with the gun. "Either shoot it or put it away," I said. "I'm staying."

She glared at me and her eyes blazed briefly. Then as suddenly as her anger had arisen, the color drained from her face, she closed her eyes and collapsed in a heap on the floor. She wasn't hard boiled at all. She was as soft as a kitten when I picked her up and put her on the divan.

I didn't forget to pick up her gun. I found the kitchen and filled a glass of water. There was a bottle of household ammonia and I brought that along, too. I revived her with the water and the ammonia and then I sat on the divan beside her and stroked her forehead. "Lie still, Tita," I said. "If you were a friend of Pete's, then you are a

28

friend of mine. Sort of inheritance. Now it appears that you need help. So we'll team up. You help me, I'll help you."

She shook her head. "Nobody can help me," she moaned.

"All right, but damn it all, I can try!"

"You swore at me!" She opened her eyes wide and looked hurt.

"You need swearing at. How the hell can I do anything for you if you get into a funk? This isn't the time for it. Where's all that defiance you had when I came in?"

She sat up and pulled down her skirts, which had pulled up over a pair of very enticing knees. "Big hero," she said. "You want to get yourself shot?"

I got up and helped her to her feet. I felt her tremble.

Then there was a low guttural voice behind me, speaking atrocious French. "Ah, the love birds!"

We sprang apart and turned, her hand finding mine. Facing us was a short, square Levantine with two stainless steel incisors and a smile as evil as fifteen-cent whisky. In his stubby right hand was a U.S. Army Colt .45. Martita was trembling again. I looked at this character in his food-stained suit and filthy shirt and I worked up a full head of steam. I yelled at him, "What do you mean, bursting in on us this way! I insist you get out of here! Get out!"

He backed a couple of steps but kept the gun pointed. "Be quiet," he said. "You'll wake the whole neighborhood."

"Get out!" I yelled. "I'll call the police!"

I advanced upon him, in the manner of an indignant tourist interrupted in his amour. He was undecided. It wouldn't seem right for him to shoot me, a foolish stranger who ignored a gun. That's what I hoped.

He held his ground and I was close enough to feel the gun in my ribs. I considered that I should try to take it away from him and now was the moment to do it. Then I considered that if it had been a dozen years ago and I had been in good shape, I would have tried to take it away from him. I backed off and a sigh escaped. "Well, what do you want?" I asked him.

He motioned with the gun and asked Martita, "Who is this type?"

Martita spoke in a husky whisper. "He is a friend of M. Dumbrowsky," she said.

The Levantine nodded as if that made everything all right and he put away his gun. I reached for the small automatic I had picked up when Martita had fainted, then thought better of it. What was the use? I wasn't going to shoot anyone.

"Why didn't you come to the villa?" he demanded of her. "We have been waiting for you."

"I—I was afraid."

"It is nearly ten o'clock," he said, pointing to a watch that nested amid the thick black hair on his wrist. "Did you think it was not important?"

She shook her head. "With M. Dumbrowsky dead. . . ."

"You do not work for M. Dumbrowsky. You work for the Baron, same as I do." He turned his head to me and showed his ugly smile. "Isn't that just like a woman? You can't depend on them."

I said, "Perhaps she doesn't want to go to the villa and see your baron. Have you thought of that?"

"But she must, monsieur!" Then he looked at me quizzically for a moment. "And what business is it of yours?"

"It occurred to me that I might help the lady do what she wants to do—and not do what she doesn't want to do. Do you follow me?"

A hurt look came into his large, moist eyes. "Is it that you do not want to see the Baron?" he asked her.

Martita shook her head. "No, I don't want to see him. I told him last week that I wouldn't see him again."

"Well, he might have told me," he exclaimed indignantly. "He said to me, 'Go get Mlle. de Castro. Don't come back here without her.' So now it turns out that you have resigned. He should have told me!"

"You go back to him and you tell him to leave me alone and to stop sending people after me."

"I certainly will!" he said. He turned and headed for the hallway. He slammed the door as he left the apartment.

I asked her, "What was that all about?"

"I worked for the Baron. Now I've quit. That's all." She sat in a corner of the divan and held her head in her hands.

30

"What's this foolishness with the gun?" I asked. "Why did he come in here with a pistol in his hand?"

"Pépé? He always carries that. He's harmless. It's unloaded. He's seen too many movies. . . ."

I took her own small automatic from my pocket and held it in my hand. She looked at it. "And this? Have you seen too many movies, too?"

She shook her head and she raised her eyes to mine. That combination of black hair and blue eyes were most disturbing to me. "No," she said seriously. "I am really afraid—of someone. If he had come to this apartment tonight, I am certain that I would have shot him."

I sat on the divan beside her and lit the cigarette I'd been wanting for a half hour. I thought about what she had said, and I thought about Pete Dumbrowsky and I smoked my cigarette, waiting for her to tell me more.

6

S HE TOLD ME A LOT, and yet it was all very little. She told me about the Baron de Lys, for whom she had worked as a sort of actuary, and I was skeptical about that because it is rare that a woman has any interest in figures and mathematics, to say nothing of being able to use them intelligently.

"But it is the truth, monsieur," she said. "I learned arithmetic from my father when I was a little girl and I have always been interested in numbers and what one can do with them. I have studied mathematics with the nuns and with the Jesuits and I spent two years at the University of Paris, up until the death of my mother."

"I will concede the point. But why does the Baron de Lys need an actuary?"

"He is a gambler, monsieur, and it is I who figure the odds for him, on everything from English football to *chemin de fer*. The Baron has run the banks at the Cannes

31

casinos for many years and often he will take over the bank at the Méditerranée and at Monte Carlo when the Greeks get hit too hard and need help. He conducts large games at his own villa during the off-seasons and he is anxious to have me around, such as now, because sometimes I can save him bad mistakes."

"And this Pépé, who arrived here with the gun?"

"You keep coming back to poor Pépé. He is harmless, I tell you. He is merely a servant in the Baron's household. I like Pépé. We are friends."

"You were frightened when he came into the room and spoke."

"I have explained that. I was not frightened of him."

"All right. Now what did Pete Dumbrowsky have to do with all of this—with the Baron and the gambling and the casinos?"

"Nothing. He was a friend of the Baron, that's all."

"And he knew Pépé?"

"Of course. All of the Baron's servants were known to M. Dumbrowsky." She got up and walked about the room. It was a pleasure to see her move and I wondered why. Then suddenly it came to me.

"You are a dancer," I said.

She whirled and looked at me. "How did you know?"

"The way you walk. The way you move."

"I studied many years with Montserre." Then she said, "You know, I am hungry. I have had no dinner."

"Neither have I."

"Then I will fix us something." She beckoned for me to follow her and went to the kitchen. I stood by the open door and watched her prepare *oeufs au plat*, hot rolls and coffee. I watched her and liked her and tried to figure what was wrong with the picture. . . . Nothing seemed to add up. There was no sense in any of the coincidences. . . . Or perhaps it was that I didn't know enough and that these were not coincidences at all. So let's start at the beginning again, I told myself.

"This is a nice apartment," I said. "Have you lived here long?"

"No. Just a few months."

"And before that?"

"Before that, I lived at the villa of Baron de Lys. I had my own apartment there and my aunt stayed with me and it was all very proper. . . . I don't know why I should tell you that. It's none of your business, really."

"Certainly it's my business," I said. "You've made it my business."

She came and faced me by the door. "Why do you say that?"

"Because you like me, just as I like you, and you must be certain that I do not misunderstand."

She tossed her head disdainfully and started to turn away. I reached out and put a hand on her shoulder. And then something or other happened—I have no clear idea what—and she was in my arms and I was kissing her. It was a nice kiss; a nice, friendly, affectionate kiss, and the earth didn't move and the sky didn't fall down and there was no sudden welling up of the grand passion. . . . She pushed me away and she said, "Yes, I do like you. But even so, we shouldn't be doing that, should we?"

"Oh," I said, "it's just a form of communication. Think nothing of it."

She looked at me out of those china-blue eyes and there was a slight frown that puckered her forehead. "It means no more to you than that?" she asked.

I shrugged at her, in the manner of a Spaniard. But nothing else I was doing was in the manner of a Spaniard. And that was no little surprise to me because I did like her and I was fully aware of the excitement of her body and the passion of her that would need so little to be aroused. Maybe I was getting obsessed with my late friend Dumbrowsky. "There is a time and a place for everything," I said. "Let's eat and talk some more and then see what happens."

"Nothing will happen," she said, turning away angrily and yanking open the oven door. "I can assure the American monsieur that nothing will happen."

Our supper à deux was tasty and satisfying in a very limited sense; otherwise it was the most unsatisfactory meal I have ever eaten. Tita had nothing to say to me beyond the minimum answers to my insistent questions. All of the friendliness, the warmth, the great potential of two persons

33

who met and liked each other immediately, were gone. I had wounded her feelings in a manner very serious to one with such pride as she possessed, and I knew it. But I was still trying to get information and I was still too single-minded to be concerned with her feelings, as I should have been. I had no conscious idea why I myself felt so unhappy about it all. The self that felt deserted and rejected wasn't functioning up on the conscious level. The self that was talking and eating and being charming, and at the same time being frightfully clever in the manner of leading the conversation into critical areas, was the machine-self that had been constructed so many years before by the geniuses of Bureau-X and had been turned loose in wartime to confound the enemy. It was the machine-self that was doing such a bad job of interesting this unusual girl.

But the end result of all my cleverness was as useless as a whistle in the wind. It dawned upon me, as we sat over a second cup of coffee, that it was just possible I was asking the wrong questions; that it didn't really matter whom she knew and had associated with, or whom she knew Dumbrowsky had associated with. There was a reason why he had known her and had asked her to send to me that final message. And the reason must lie within herself, rather than in the external world in which she lived.

"Like most Americans," I said, "I am afraid of love. We are brought up that way, to regard love as something sinister and forbidden—something nasty. Outwardly, we all get over this notion at an early age, as soon as we find out what love really is composed of, but there is always that residue of fear at trespassing and sinning, and so we Americans very often mess up our associations with women, and especially with European women."

"How interesting."

"What I am trying to do is to apologize to you for my boorishness."

"No apology is necessary. I was not aware of any misbehavior."

"But I like you, Tita. I like you tremendously."

"So?"

"So, I want you to like me."

She sat looking at me. There was no expression on her

34

face. It seemed that I had sure enough broken my plate.

"What do your friends call you?" she asked finally. It was the first hopeful thing she had said. She was interested enough to want to know my name.

"A very few friends—less than five—call me Alex."

"Alex, for Alexander?"

"No, for Alexis. The Russian influence."

"You are not Russian?"

"No. My mother was American but my father was Russian. Back in the bad old days of the Czars he had been sort of chancellor of the exchequer for Nicholas. He was on a diplomatic mission and we were all in Washington when the Revolution broke out."

She nodded her head as though she understood a lot more than I had said. Some of the opaque indifference left her eyes. "My father was Don Carlos Ortega de Castro-y-Lomas."

"Should I know who he is?" I asked.

She shook her head. "No. He is well forgotten now. He was the Minister of the Treasury for the Republican Government of Spain."

"That is a coincidence," I said. "We come from the same stock of treasury robbers."

Her eyes flashed at me and she jumped from her chair. "That is an insult!" she said. She stood glaring at me, hands on her hips, legs apart, ready for battle.

I got out of my chair slowly and faced her. "In America that is no insult," I said. "It is just a pleasantry. We use such outrageous characterizations of our parents because we love them. . . . It would be the same as though I called you a little bitch right now."

"What do you mean!"

"This." I moved in quickly and took her in my arms. I pressed my lips on hers and held her tightly so that she could not move. She started to bite my lower lip and she brought a hand up to scratch my face. Then as suddenly as her struggle began it ended and she was kissing me with a fire that singed the edges of my being. You would not have called it a nice, friendly, affectionate kiss. There was passion and hunger and pain and wanting in it, and she pressed her slim, supple body so close to mine that we

35

were one. No, the earth didn't move, yet, nor did the sky fall down, but these phenomena were right on the edge of happening.

Then she led me into her bedroom, which was as severe as a nun's cell, with the single exception of the large double bed, and we lay down crosswise on the bed in each other's arms and we kissed long.

After awhile she raised up on her elbow and she said in a voice so low that I could just hear, "Now you may undress me. But I want you to undress me slowly, just a bit at a time, and I want you to kiss me all over as you do. . . . I will tell you exactly how I want you to make love to me, and then I want you to tell me exactly how you want me to make love to you. . . . I have been thinking about this for a long time and I have been thinking about you for a long time, waiting for you to come into my life. Now that you are here, you will do exactly as I wish and I will do exactly as you wish. . . . Darling! I love you!"

So I did exactly as she wished. . . .

Along about ten o'clock the next morning she woke me up with a kiss and had coffee and *croissants* at the bedside on a tray. She wore nothing but a smock that just barely covered the V of her sex when she stood up. Also, when she stood up, her small, perfect breasts pushed out the smock in a most enticing way. . . . "Last night you were magnificent," she said, handing me the coffee and sitting on the edge of the bed. "You made love to me the way I have always dreamed of being loved—and to think! You are an American!"

"Well, we do it in America, too, and some of us learn a thing or two."

"I would not have believed it. And when you held me thus and you put your hand here. . . ." and she proceeded to discuss fully and in the most minute detail the entire course of our *amour*, in the manner of the French girls, who always insist on such post mortems after the act of love. I listened to her carefully and I drank my coffee and I ate a *croissant*, and then I pulled her into bed beside me again and the discussion was smothered in deeds. . . . At noon we opened our eyes together and she said, "Darling, let us just stay here in bed as long as we can—until we are driven out by hunger."

I said, "It's all right with me, sweetheart."

"Do you think me shameless?"

"Of course. You are a shameless hussy."

"What!"

"You are the most delightfully shameless hussy I've ever known."

"Just a roll in the hay, maybe. . . ."

"Not unless you want it that way."

"But you don't know me at all. We've known each other for only a few hours."

"I've known you all of my life. I've known you exactly— the size of you and the feel of you and the smell of you. . . . The mere fact that we didn't meet sooner is just an unfortunate incident."

"Do you really mean that?"

"Yes."

"Will you tell me something?"

"Anything."

"Do you love me?"

"Yes, darling, I love you. I hope it becomes the greatest love I have ever known."

"Ummm. You do say the nicest things."

"Will you tell me something?"

"Maybe."

"Did you have an affair with Pete Dumbrowsky?"

"Why do you ask?"

"I'm hunting for something. I don't know what it is, but it may be very important. If you had an affair with him, then perhaps I'm hunting in the wrong place."

"It's none of your business, but I didn't. I am not promiscuous. I will not sleep with a man unless I have a very strong feeling for him. I had no feeling for M. Dumbrowsky."

"Then what was it?"

"What was what?"

"Why did he—" then suddenly it came to me—"Why did he put you up in this apartment?"

"He didn't 'put me up,' as you term it. He knew that I had to leave the villa, after my aunt became ill and

37

went to the hospital. He told me he would find a place for me and he did. This place. And I pay the rent."

"He spent much time with you here, didn't he?"

"Of course. We were good friends and often he would come and cook dinner for us. You know that he was an excellent chef?"

"Yes, I knew that. Did he like to look out of the window?"

"What a silly question! . . . But now that you mention it, he did. He moved the dining table by the window, where it is now, and for long periods he would seem to be preoccupied with the—the outdoors."

"The hotel across the courtyard?"

"Perhaps. It never occurred to me to wonder."

"I think we are getting somewhere," I said. I got out of bed and began to dress. "Will you come to Cannes with me?"

"You are *not* going to Cannes! You are going to stay here!" She jumped out of bed and took my head in her hands. "Please, Alex, don't go away."

"You will go with me."

"But I want us to stay here," she wailed. "I want us to stay until—until—"

"I know," I said, kissing her gently, "but right now we are going to Cannes. So get your clothes on."

7

I RETRIEVED the Simca from the hotel garage and we drove to Cannes, along the Corniche. As we approached Le Trayas Tita said, "That's the villa."

She was pointing to the huge palace I had noted on my way to St. Raphael—where the blonde and the redhead had come swerving out of the driveway. Where the redhead had made the gesture to me with her hand that might have been obscene, in the manner of the Italians.

38

"The Baron de Lys must be very wealthy to maintain such an establishment in these days," I remarked.

"He's got all the money there is," she said. "We used to live here."

"You!"

"Yes. It originally belonged to my father—but it didn't look like this, I can tell you. It was a big barn of a place then, all caving in. . . . We sold it right after he died and it has been entirely rebuilt, from the foundation up. They spent a fortune on it, and I've always wondered why. They could have started from scratch with a nice new piece of wilderness and built le Trayas for half the money."

"What about this Baron de Lys," I persisted. "What's his background?"

"He married the old baroness—she was twice his age —and when she died he inherited everything including the title. He'd had himself adopted by her when they got married, so he'd be her legal heir—husband and son all rolled into one. He's a Corsican—a *maquereau* type, really. He's too oily for me. I can't stand him as a man, but he was a friend of my father and he has treated me extremely well. It's just that—well, he did try to make love to me once."

"Just once?"

"I was very emphatic. I scratched his face so badly that he did not appear for two weeks."

I drove along in silence for several kilometers, thinking about the Corsican baron and his rich, elderly wife who had died, and, of course, of Martita. She was sitting close to me and I could feel the warmth of her at my shoulder.

"You mentioned the Greeks," I said. "You told me that this de Lys bails them out at the casinos when their banks go sour. Don't you know these Greeks are the wealthiest men in the world today?"

"Oh yes, I have heard so, but their wealth is as nothing compared to the funds the Baron has available."

"Are you certain?"

"Of course. I have kept his accounts for nearly a year."

"It is odd that he should have so much. I've never even heard of him, and it is my business to know of wealthy men."

"You have not heard of the Baroness either?"

39

"Yes, she was around before and during the War, when I was over here. But I do not remember that her riches were extraordinary. . . . The Baron must have other sources than her fortune."

"Perhaps. He keeps them well hidden."

"And you will not work for him further?"

"No. I have had enough."

"Will you tell me why?"

She shook her head. "It has nothing to do with you or with the Baron either, for that matter."

"Will you tell me a name?"

"What name, dearest?"

"Of the man whom you fear?"

She didn't answer. We drove the winding road to Theoule and then through la Napoule-les-Bains. I held her hand and every once in a while she would squeeze mine with surprising strength. Finally she said, "He was at the Hotel Nouvel the last time I saw him. He drove up in his car as I was passing and got out to go into the hotel. He saw me and he stopped me and he asked me to come with him and have lunch." A shiver passed through her body.

"What is his name?" I asked.

She was silent for another little time, then she said, "That was only yesterday. It seems like a year ago—so much has happened to me since yesterday. . . . Well, yes, I will tell you his name. It is Vico del Oro."

It was my turn to be silent. This was a name I had known very well in the *maquis* around Grasse. Vico del Oro had been one of the great "heroes" of the *maquis* and had been credited with magnificent feats of daring when Corsica was occupied by the Italians and Germans. It had been said that he had turned over a considerable fortune to the cause—although some skeptics had opined that he had got ten francs back for every one he donated as a result of his black-market operations. There had been whispers that he controlled the black markets from Marsilles to Menton.

"Do you know him?" she asked.

"Yes, in a way. I saw him during the War."

"He is a slimy snail of a man. He has dead eyes that

look at you and kill you too. He is all evil—Alex, he is the most frightening person I have ever known!"

"And he is a friend of the Baron de Lys?"

"A close friend. They are like brothers. The Baron has insisted that I be nice to him. Lately he would have him around all the time, and I would have to eat with him and be with him even when I worked. It was too much!"

That intelligence took us to the outskirts of Cannes. We stopped for a traffic light. I leaned over and kissed her on the cheek. That wasn't good enough. She made it a real kiss, and the driver behind us honked his horn because the light had changed to green.

I got under way again. I said, "What was the name of de Lys before he took the title of his wife?"

She said a name that, somehow, I was not surprised to hear, another of the Arbori clan. "His name was Aldo Arbori."

I had come to Cannes in search of Bureau-X—or rather, to let Bureau-X find me. I assumed that they would assume I had departed the Hotel Beau Sejour when I learned of Dumbrowsky's death. I assumed that they would assume I would come to Cannes, where Fat Mildred had given me the Simca and had bid adieu. It was all safe enough assuming on my part. I had been with those spy-chasers long enough to know how their minds worked.

What I wanted to find out was what Bureau-X knew of Pete's death, if anything. What I wanted to know was what they were going to do about it. I knew what I was going to try to do about it, but I had just enough respect for them not to want to run afoul of their efforts. If they were going to make any efforts.

I registered at the Hotel Martinez with Tita as Mr. and Mrs. Randall McCarey of Virginia, U.S.A., and we went up to a large room overlooking the Mediterranean. Cannes was livelier than St. Raphael this early in the season and the winter's peeling paint was not so much in evidence, but even so it was a dead resort compared to what lay ahead.

Tita said, "Well! A bed!"

"You keep out of it," I said. "We've got business to do."

41

"That's what I was thinking of. Business."

I took her in my arms and I kissed her. Then I sat her down in a chair by the window and I knelt on the floor at her feet.

"Listen, sex-bucket, we're waiting for some people. They're liable to show up any minute. I've got to see them. So let's keep our pants on."

She sat there smouldering, her china eyes looking through me. I got to feeling the way she did and it wouldn't have been more than a few minutes before she would have won that round. But there was a knock on the door. I yelled, *"Entrez!"* and Fat Mildred came bouncing in. Perhaps bounce isn't the word. What she did, whenever she walked, was jiggle.

"Hello, boy friend," she greeted, closing the door behind her. Then she saw Tita and she stood there with her mouth open. But sounds still came out. They were: "And Mlle. de Castro! Imagine finding you here!"

I said, "It's convenient not to have to bother with introductions. Well, honey, what's the scoop?"

"Updyke is in 1140-A and B, jittering between the two and waiting for you. All hell's broken loose and you're the goat. Something to do with your libido."

I said, "That nasty tongue of yours is going to get you slugged one of these days." I leaned over and kissed Tita. She was sitting with her eyes down, not paying any attention to us. She returned my kiss, but coolly.

"I'll see you shortly," I told her. "Wait for me."

Then I left the room, brushing by Fat Mildred as she stood near the door. "Keep an eye on her," I growled.

I took the elevator to the eleventh floor and entered 1140-B without knocking. It was a sitting room, nicely furnished and with a radio near the door blaring a jazz concert. I banged the door shut so that it would be heard. Updyke came in from the bedroom wearing a wine-colored velvet smoking jacket and chewing an extra-long panatella. He was dressed for the cigar, sure enough.

He walked over and locked the door I had entered, turned the radio down a decible and a half, then stuck out his hand for me to shake. I shook.

"We've got about fifteen minutes," he said. "Your

42

plane is being gassed up at the airport. You can make connections at Orly for the Pan-American flight home this evening."

"The hell I can!"

"The—what?"

"I'm not ready to leave."

"See here, Bodine, we're not going to stand for any more nonsense from you. You'll be on that plane if we have to carry you aboard in a basket."

I laughed. One short "Ha!" "How about Pete Dumbrowsky?" I asked.

"What about him? He's dead."

"I saw his body just after he landed."

"That finishes it, so far as you are concerned."

"That finishes nothing. It begins it."

"No. We brought you over here for a specific reason. Now the reason has been removed and we will conduct our activities in our own way, without you."

"I am not satisfied that your activities will be in the best interests of the late Mr. Dumbrowsky. You indicated to me, back in Virginia, that he was in some danger, and it was for that reason that I agreed to undertake this expedition. Now the danger has resulted in the ultimate. Pete is dead. He was murdered."

Updyke shook his head and smiled. In a superior way. "No, Pete was not murdered. He was in no danger," he said. "I can tell you that now. I admit that I am guilty of a degree of misrepresentation, but it seemed important then to get you to do what we wanted."

"And his death in the courtyard?"

"Unfortunate. Very unfortunate for us. But it was either an accident, which seems highly probable, or he took his own life for reasons unknown. You cannot dramatize that incident into a murder, my friend."

"I know what I know. He was defenestrated, in the classic manner. He didn't have accidents and he certainly didn't kill himself. He told this de Castro girl, 'If anything happens to me, send a message to M. McCarey.' He would not have told her that unless he expected that something *might* happen to him. And the something that might

43

happen would prevent him from seeing me, as planned. So it happened. He was killed."

Updyke grimaced at me. "There is no evidence to support that view. That's not the way we heard it."

"Then you haven't heard anything. You been listening to Delacroix?"

"Of the *Sûreté*? Yes, he was here a half an hour ago."

"I would have guessed. The *Sûreté* is tied up in this somewhere. Or at least Delacroix is. He went to a lot of trouble to find out if I was Alex Bodine. There's a crooked policeman if I ever saw one. . . . You want to tell me what Dumbrowsky was working on?"

"No. You're not with us any more, Bodine. You'll just have to go back home. We don't want you around."

"You remember Dottie?" I asked.

"Yes, I remember Mrs. Bodine."

"She was killed in an automobile accident. Another car ran hers off the road. It was all neat and reasonable and regrettable—except that they never did find the driver of the other car, which had a phony registration and a stolen engine. I couldn't find this man either. You know why? Because Bureau-X didn't want me to. Bureau-X said it was an accident and that I should mind my own business. I'll tell you something. Dottie was murdered."

"Well?"

"Now we come to Pete Dumbrowsky. He was a friend of mine. He was as close to me, once, in his own way as Dottie was in hers. So once again Bureau-X tells me to mind my own business. Once again Bureau-X tells me there was no murder. You know what I think? I think you are a bunch of knuckleheads. I think your organization has gone plumb to hell since old General Deschines died. So I'm going to find out about Pete. And if you try to stop me, I'm going to be a lot of trouble. More trouble than you can handle. Do we understand each other?"

He nodded. "Yes, but nevertheless you'll be on that plane."

"Let's talk some more first. What about this Martita de Castro. Fat Mildred had something to say about her."

"It doesn't make any difference now. We thought of

44

using you—that is, if you so desired—but not after your night with Martita. She's on the wrong side."

"The wrong side of what?"

"Do you know who her father was?"

"Yes, she told me."

"He was the Minister of the Treasury of the Spanish Republican Government. In October, 1936, he personally turned over to the Russian Government the gold of said treasury."

"That's a sin, I guess," I said. "As I recall, the money was supposed to have bought arms."

"We have no quarrel with that part of the transaction. But the official report issued some time later was that the Republican Treasury had contained one billion, seven hundred thirty-four million gold pesetas, which amounts to about $570 million. However, the Russians never got $570 million. They have produced manifests and receipts for only $560 million. So somebody got away with $10 million."

"Who? De Castro?"

"Probably not. . . . We got interested when this discrepancy came to light because such a sum of money could buy off a lot of people for purposes of espionage. We wanted to make certain that it was not in the wrong hands. Our investigations then disclosed the amazing fact that all of the records had been tampered with—that there was no truth in any of them. We now have reason to believe that the Spanish Republican Treasury contained almost three billion gold pesetas and that the total amount unaccounted for is close to $360 million in gold."

"So De Castro buried his gold out in the back yard of his villa and lived happy ever after. Now the sins of the father are visited upon the daughter, I suppose."

"The daughter," he said solemnly, "has all of the records. At least we think she has. And if she has, she alone knows how much gold there was. She would then be the only one left alive who could prove it."

"And she won't tell Bureau-X? Good for her!"

"It wouldn't be very good for her if somebody wanted these records badly enough to kill her for them. Now we don't think that's necessarily the case, only a possibility. We think that these records have been well hidden so that killing her would not produce them. We believe that arrangements have been made so that if anything does happen to Martita de Castro, then the records will be revealed. It is more logical that way. It would protect her and it would protect the records."

"It sounds like melodramatic nonsense to me," I said. "Who would want to keep such records? Not De Castro. He's dead. And certainly not Martita. If she had an ounce of sense, she'd know they were dynamite—that she'd have to get rid of them. No, I don't buy your story at all, Updyke."

"I admit we are just guessing about this. Pete Dumbrowsky told us most of it, and he frankly didn't know the truth from the fiction. He told us that this Martita had left the employment of Baron de Lys suddenly and mysteriously. He told us that she seemed to be deathly afraid of someone or something. That's all he knew about it and that's all we know about it. The rest we are deducing. . . . However, there are plenty of other facts which support our deductions. In the first place, there is a tremendous sum of money involved and any persons who obtained control of these hundreds of millions would automatically assume great power and prestige. They would not want to have their respectability attacked and they would use their power ruthlessly to guard it. Now it is inevitable that this gold was obtained fraudulently from De Castro. Otherwise the transaction would have been recorded somewhere. So if the records would reveal that fraud, then the threat is multiplied. No, my boy, they wouldn't want Martita de Castro around to testify against them at all."

"If she knows anything," I said.

"Oh, she knows. And no woman is discreet with her lovers. All she would have to do to blow the lid off would be to whisper her little tale into the ear of a bedroom companion—"

"Nuts," I interrupted. "In the first place, she's not that kind of girl at all!"

He shook his head at me. "You never change, Bodine. You are the perennial romantic. You fall in love with every girl you sleep with, and she becomes a pure flower, untouched before you came along. It is your one great weakness."

"I'm not wrong about Martita," I insisted. "I've gotten to know her very well in this short time and I'm as certain of what kind of girl she is as I am certain that you wouldn't know a decent woman from a whore anywhere. . . . However, I don't see where any of this puts her on the wrong side of Bureau-X."

"There are two sides to every question and to every spy hunt. Naturally we are on the trail of the enemy—the Russians. How they are mixed up in this is none of your business. Martita could have helped us. Instead she helped the other side. Does that answer you?"

"Maybe. I'll have to find out for myself."

"You'll find out nothing." He looked at his watch. "We'd better get under way."

I had Tita's little automatic in my hand pointing at his head. I said, "Lean against the wall, Colonel, feet apart and weight resting on the palms of your hands. . . . You know how."

He looked shocked and he said, "You wouldn't shoot me, you know." But he did as he was told. He got into position and I got myself a beautiful Magnum from a shoulder holster and extra shells in a small box in his coat pocket. I kept him covered with his Magnum and locked the door to the bedroom. Then I told him he could relax and sit down.

He sat. He scowled at me and he said, "I don't know what you hope to gain by this. You are acting like a fool. What good is it going to do you to remain on the Riviera, against our wishes? You'll not only have us against you— you'll have to fight the *Sûreté* and *gendarmerie*."

"I don't think so," I said. "I don't think you'll alert the French police—unless Bureau-X has completely changed its mode of operation. Would you like me to tell the French why you brought me over here?"

"It wouldn't make any difference," he said. "You don't know anything yet."

I shook my head at him. "Don't jump to conclusions," I said. "I've been here long enough to learn a little. Do you want me to tell you about the Hotel Nouvel and the Baron de Lys and Vico del Oro? Do you want to know what Pete Dumbrowsky was doing in Martita de Castro's flat every night? Do you want to know who Sandor Barodi is? ... Maybe I do know a little."

He sat looking at me, his face expressionless, playing poker, betting on his hand which held at least a pair of deuces.

"I'm going to keep out of your way," I continued. "I'm going to do what I think I have to do, then I'm going home. You don't have to worry about me—about what side I'm on. I'll even tell you what I've found out before I leave, if you want to listen. But get one thing straight, I'm going to put a bullet through the head of the guy that got Pete Dumbrowsky." I pointed to the middle of my forehead. "Right here."

"That's nonsense," he said. "Nobody 'got' Pete Dumbrowsky, as you like to put it. . . . You middle-aged romantics give me a headache."

"Middle-aged!" I exclaimed. I looked down at my pot, which I noted had grown less in this short time. Then I straightened my shoulders. "You've got a short memory, Updyke. You choose to ignore the fact that a very few short years ago I went into Russia and that I delivered. I realize you were no part of that deal, but surely you've heard about it. Surely it's no secret now that I was the assassin for Bureau-X, that I killed—"

"Yes, yes," he interrupted impatiently, "I've heard all about that. You're tough, all right. You're as tough as they come—in your own league. But in this league over here, you're nothing but a pansy."

I laughed at him. I shook the Magnum at him. I said, "I've got an equalizer now, Updyke. There's nobody tougher than one of these hunks of lead." I started for the door.

"You're welcome to the Magnum," he said. "I hope it does you some good. You can use the Simca, too, if you wish."

"No thanks," I said. "I'll get a car—one that won't be known to every Bureau-X punk and cop in Provence."

I walked out the door and down the hall to the elevator.

I admitted to myself that I'd been wrong about Updyke. He wasn't such a bad joe, once you got the drop on him with his own gun.

8

I WENT DOWN to the hotel lobby and I called my room. Tita answered the phone. "Are you alone?" I asked.

"Yes."

"That's bad. Somebody's cooking up something or they wouldn't leave you alone. Where's Mildred?"

"She'll be back. Where are you?"

"In the lobby. Come right down. I'll be in front in a cab. Hurry."

"But darling! I—"

"Hurry, Tita, do you hear? This is urgent! Nothing else matters! Don't waste a minute!"

I hung up, went out and got the doorman to get me a taxi. He called up a small Puegeot from the head of the line and I squeezed into the back seat. It wasn't easy. "Wait a moment," I told the driver, "I've got a friend coming."

We waited. Three minutes went by. The driver turned off the engine. A party came out of the hotel, two elderly dames in pastels and minks and a young gigolo with a thin moustache and tight pants. They got into a Rolls ahead of us, the dames giggling and the gigolo smiling in a forced way and showing his white teeth. Three more minutes went by. The driver swung his head around and gave me a questioning look. "These women," I said. He nodded. He understood. He slouched down to get comfortable. I looked out at the deserted beach. It was a bleak day, the kind of a day that makes you disagreeable to strangers and unpredictable with your friends. Three more minutes. I opened the door and got out to stretch my legs. I could see into the hotel hall. Tita was just beyond the door. A man in a dark gray suit and black homburg was talking to her. Two other men in dark suits flanked her. They had cop written all over them. The man talking was emphasizing a point with his hands, as Frenchmen do. He turned his head enough for me to see his profile. It was Delacroix of the *Sûreté*. I debated for a second whether I should go in and try to get her. Not more than a second. I turned quickly and went back to the taxi. I got in and told the driver, "Let's get going. She isn't coming."

He started the engine, put the car in gear and took off. "Where to, monsieur?"

"Turn left on the boulevard. I'll tell you when to stop."

We went along la Croisette towards the Palm Beach Casino. I had once known this road very well. I had a clear memory that there was a large garage not too far along. It was closer than I had remembered, beside a railway overpass. "Turn left here and take me to the rue d'Antibes," I said.

I got out at the corner of the avenue de Madrid, paid the driver, then walked back to the garage. It was a Citroën agency and the manager turned out to be a round and debonnaire Frenchman with an optimistic outlook. I told him, "I want a car for a week or so, monsieur. I am willing to pay very well."

"Ah, that is what I like to hear in this business," he said. "I would presume you would want one of our new models. It just so happens that we have—"

I interrupted him with a hand on his arm. "No, monsieur, not a new model. An old one will do very well. I don't want to impress anybody. I just want to ride around."

"A very amusing notion," he said. "Well, all right. We will give you what you desire."

I made a deal for a 1954 sedan in good condition at three thousand francs per day and I gave him fifty thousand francs in crisp, new bills so that he would not insist upon seeing my papers and upon references. "We will make this deal under a tree in Switzerland," I said. "Actually, I have lost my papers—but I should have them back in a week."

"You speak excellent French, monsieur, but the accent eludes me. May I ask your nationality?"

"Czechoslovakian," I said. I got into the car and drove

off, leaving him beaming after me. I drove the inland route to Frejus, then back to St. Raphael and the rue Honoré-Vadon. I still had the key to Tita's flat, given to me by the concierge for my six thousand francs, and I went past the concierge's lodge unobserved and up the stairs. The key opened the door this time without hindrance. I closed the door, jammed the chair under the handle as she had done, then began a search of the apartment. It was a thorough search. There was no single thing that Tita had touched, worn, or looked at that was not examined inside and out, and that included the pictures on the walls, the drapes, the floorboards, and her wearing apparel.

I found little enough of interest. There were two identical keys on a small chain. They were long and thin, of a most unusual shape, and appeared to have been hand made by an excellent craftsman. On each was stamped the number 568. They had been wrapped in paper and pasted to the bottom of a bureau drawer. The paper that enclosed them was a receipt for one thousand three hundred-fifty francs from the *Credit Paris-Sud* at Hyères. The third item was a one hundred-franc note issued in 1943 by the Bank of Algiers and printed in Philadelphia. It had been very carefully hidden in the leather binding of Thomas à Kempis, printed in London 1897 by Arthur L. Humphreys. I opened à Kempis at random, as one is supposed to do, and I hit Chapter V on page 121 and the next paragraph began, "Love is watchful, and sleeping slumbereth not. Though weary, it is not tired; though pressed, it is not straightened; though alarmed, it is not confounded; but as a lively flame and burning torch, it forces its way upwards, and securely passes them all."

So I sat down for awhile and thought about Tita— about whether Bureau-X was right or I was right; about whether she loved me or was using me. . . . In all good sense, how could she love me after having known me such a few hours, even as I had known her? Did I love her? Could I love her in so short a period, no matter what emotional and passionate experiences we had shared? And then, of course, there was the final question of capacity, on her part as well as on mine. Was either of us capable of a deep love of lasting significance? I had once been certain that I was, before I had married Dottie. But after Dottie and I had lived together for a year, I began to doubt myself. I found that I was changing; I found that I was becoming critical of her in strange ways; I believed that I was seeing her clearly for the first time and that I was discovering Dottie was not the girl I had thought at all. . . . Was it that my love had waned and wavered so that I could take her or leave her? It was a frightening thought and I had put it from me forcefully, but it had returned time and time again.

It had returned up until the time of her death, and then I was sure for the first time that this had not been a valid doubt at all. But then it was too late to be sure. . . . Now Tita. Despite the cynical view of Colonel Updyke, I had never been deeply involved with the girls with whom I had had affairs. I had spoken about them with enthusiasm, of course, and I had done other foolish things because of them, but I was never in love with them. I was in love with the loving, yes, but not with the girls. But with Tita it was different. Even in so short a time it was different. I knew then that I wanted Tita with me whether we made love or not. I knew that she had everything I was seeking in a woman, just as Dottie had had. I knew—

There was a knocking at the door of the flat. It was an authoritative knocking, as though the knockee was confident of admittance, or of a right to admittance. I walked quietly down the hall and removed the chair, making as little noise as possible. Then I took out Updyke's Magnum and opened the door. There stood before me a dark, handsome youth of about twenty-five. He had black curls and chiseled features and a bearing of grace and pride—a good-looking boy with a good face. He said, in musical Andalusian, "Who the hell are you?"

I replied in my San Antonio gutter Mexican, "Come in, my friend. I am an associate of Señorita de Castro."

I kept the gun down by my leg and he didn't see it. He walked past me and into the living room. I closed the door, pocketed the gun, and followed him.

"Can you speak French or English?" I asked him. "My Spanish smells."

He looked at me unsmiling, then glanced around the

52

room. Nothing was out of place—I had cleaned up after myself as I went along. He said in French, "I am hunting for Martita. Where is she?"

"I don't know. Cannes, maybe. I don't think she'll come back here. Not for a long time."

He bit his lip and walked over to the window and looked out. Every movement and gesture was careful, as though studied—in dramatic school. Now he was in a mood of deep thought. You could not mistake that it was a mood of deep thought.

"Have you thought much about Hollywood?" I asked.

"Who wants Hollywood? I'm not interested in those cheap, commercial ventures!"

"But they pay well."

He sighed. "Yes, the money would be nice. But you see, there is no way I can call myself to their attention, unless I get some big parts over here, or else go to Broadway. . . . It is a difficult problem."

"If you can speak English well enough, Broadway might certainly use you."

"Oh, I can speak English well enough," he said in English. He spoke with a Brooklyn accent that was as authentic as the Bowanus Canal. "Martita was going to help me. She had expected to come into a large hunk of cash from her mother's estate along about now."

"Is that so? I hadn't heard about that."

"Oh yes. Her mother was my aunt."

"Is that so. . . . That makes you Tita's cousin."

"Yes, I am Pedro Lomas. Tita and I were brought up together. Our families settled here in France after the fighting in Spain. Were you in the Civil War?"

"No, it was a little before my time. Tell me, where did you learn your English?"

"I worked for an American gentleman for two years. I drove his car and did other chores. He taught me."

"He was from Brooklyn?"

"No, he was from Newark, New Jersey. Do you know him, Mr. Joseph Campo?"

"No, I don't know Joe Campo. But I bet he had two Cadillacs and a villa overlooking the Mediterranean."

Pedro laughed. "You are right about the Cadillacs. But

53

he was a guest of the Baron de Lys for a long time. I think when he comes back this spring he will buy his own villa, though."

"That figures. . . . Are you working now, Pedro?"

"No. I have prospects—but, nothing."

I looked at him. Tita's cousin—a good face. Probably just what I needed. "Would you like to work for me? I need someone like you, but it is highly confidential work and it would have to be someone I could trust."

"You could trust me, sir."

"Do you know how to use a gun or a knife?"

"I am very good with a knife," he said smiling. "Look." He raised his right arm suddenly and there was a knife in his hand. It was a long, thin blade and he held it in a manner that would have been efficient in attack.

"You go around prepared, eh?"

"We Lomas have many enemies. . . . Martita taught me this trick. She is the best I have ever seen with a knife."

"That may be, but at the critical moment she faints. . . . Well, you're hired. Three thousand francs a day and expenses—meals, hotel, etc. The first thing I need is some money. Go find me a Swiss banker who is to be trusted and who sells francs. I will pay the black market rate, plus a reasonable percent for himself if he insists. I will give him a check on an American bank."

"How much will you need?"

"About a thousand dollars worth."

"Good. . . . But sir, I should know your name, shouldn't I?"

"McCarey," I said. "Randall McCarey." He offered me his hand, announcing his own name formally, and we shook.

"I'll be back within an hour," he said.

I followed Pedro out. I stopped at the concierge's *loge* and told her that Mlle. de Castro had given me permission to use her flat while she was away and that I would keep the key. I gave her another thousand francs—one of my last notes—and then went on out and to the corner where there was a *tabac*. I bought a handful of telephone *jetons* and I called the Martinez Hotel in Cannes.

First I asked the operator for my room. There was a long ringing and no answer. That figured. Then I asked for the room of Mlle. Mildred Browne.

"We have no Mlle. Browne," she said.

"It is the American mademoiselle," I explained. "Perhaps she is using her married name—although she has separated from him, you understand. She is a large girl—one would call her fat."

"Ah, perhaps monsieur refers to Mme. Corbin?"

"Yes, that sounds like it. Would you ring her room?"

"Of a certainty." There were two rings and then a familiar voice answered. *"Oui? J'écoute."*

"Where's Martita?" I asked without any preliminaries.

"Where are you?"

"Never mind. Where is she?"

"Delacroix took her."

"I know that. Where did he take her?"

"To Grasse, I guess. The *Sûreté* is getting very active."

"You want to help me?"

"No."

"Will you help me then?"

"Maybe. What's on your mind?"

"Martita. Will you call the *sous-préfecture* and find out if she's there? I'll call you back in ten minutes."

"O.K. for old time's sake, I'll make one phone call."

I went to the bar and ordered a coffee. I was starving but adamant. Well, fairly adamant. I poked my stomach a couple of times, then took a hard-boiled egg from a bowl and shelled it with great care. I ate it slowly, drinking my coffee in small sips, without sugar or milk. I felt very virtuous. I kept track of the time and extended my meal to cover the ten minutes. Then I went back down the stairs to the telephone, which was alongside the door to the men's room and smelled strongly of urine. I got the Hotel Martinez quickly and then Mildred.

"What's the word?"

"She's not at the *sous-préfecture*," she said. "She was there but she left with Delacroix a half an hour ago."

"Any idea where they'd be going?"

"If I know that one, they'd be going to a hotel."

"Nuts," I said. "You don't know that one."

55

"Well, what do you think, boy friend?"

"Something's cooking. I'm going to make some assumptions and I'm going to a certain place and I'm going to find her. You think I don't know how to detect, you're crazy."

"Good luck, sap."

" 'Bye, lover."

I went back to No. 8 and rang for the concierge. She came to the window munching bread. But she was skinny so it didn't matter. I gave her the key to the apartment and told her to give it to M. Lomas when he came in and tell him to wait for me. "I'll be back in a couple of hours," I said.

Then I went out, got in the Citroën, and drove the Corniche towards Cannes. I stopped just beyond Le Trayas, on the right hand side of the road in a spot where I could see cars coming the other way for half a mile. I lit a cigarette and sat back to wait.

I didn't think I was wrong. Something was going on and a large part of it concerned Martita de Castro. They wanted her back at the villa. "They" were the Baron and his friends. First they had sent Pépé, but that had fouled up. Then they had sent Delacroix, to make it appear official and also to allay her fears. Delacroix would have taken her to the *sous-préfecture* first and ask her questions of some sort or another, then made her sign a paper. All that would be so much window dressing. Then he would have offered to drive her to the villa, or he would have told her that he must take her to the villa if she seemed reluctant. . . .

That's a large chunk of assuming, I concede. But it was the only course of events that would make sense. Otherwise Martita would have joined me in the cab in front of the Martinez. There had been no doubt of the urgency in my voice when I had spoken to her. And there could be no doubt of her own desire, if last night meant anything at all.

Not many cars passed. One small panel truck from a laundry, an English Rover loaded with kids and driven by an elderly dame, a Bentley all fancied up and driven by a uniformed chauffeur. . . . A Citroën, the twin of mine, approached from around the far turn. I started my engine and put the car into gear. I waited tensely, the Magnum on the seat beside me. The Citroën came at a good clip and about fifty feet from me I could see that there was only one person in the front seat. I turned off my engine. The car whizzed by and a grim-faced ancient in a straw hat gave me a curious glance. I settled down to wait some more. In the next fifteen minutes only one car passed, a T.R.-2 occupied by a couple of tourists. Then another Citroën hove into view and I started my engine again. This time I could detect two persons in the front seat when it got close enough. I waited, my hands gripping the wheel. It passed going fast, Delacroix driving and Martita sitting beside him. Neither glanced at me. I swung around sharply, the tires squealing. I stepped hard on the accelerator and as Delacroix slowed down for Le Trayas I was tailgating him. We went through the town that way and then he tried to pull away from me. There was a straight stretch of road ahead. I put the gas pedal to the floor and pulled out to go around him. At first it appeared that he was not going to let me pass, then he pulled over and slowed down a bit. I pulled slightly ahead of him. There was an angry look on his face as he saw me for the first time. I swung to the right to force him either to stop or to hit me. He jammed on his brakes.

He yelled something at me. I think he would have tried to out-run me but I had forced him so far over that he could not get back on the road without stopping to let me pass. He stopped and I stopped, the front of my car across his. I jumped out, the Magnum in my hand. He started to back away and I pointed the gun at him. He came to a stop again and I walked over to his side of the car.

I spoke to Martita. "Get in my car," I told her. "Drive it slowly towards St. Raphael. Stop this side of the town if we don't catch up with you before."

"O.K.," was all she said. I waited until she had gone a hundred yards down the road. Then I walked around and got into the seat beside Delacroix.

He said nothing. No expostulations. No threats. No indignation. Just that tired, old-world look and a cynical smile. I said, "Do you want to drive on?"

He put the car in gear and got under way.

"Drive slowly," I said.

He nodded again. Then he said, "You are this Alexis Bodine, aren't you?"

"Yes," I said.

"I had to make certain—that's why I've let you get away with this outrageous performance. Do you think we of the *Sûreté* can't cope with your childish, American gangster methods?"

"You could try," I said. "You sure as hell could try."

He laughed. "I could have a force of a hundred men here within minutes!" He pointed to the two-way radio on the dash. "That is no toy, my friend."

I hefted the Magnum. "This isn't either. It speaks much more direct than a radio. I wouldn't hesitate to kill you, Delacroix. You or anyone else who got in my way. The great *Sûreté Générale* doesn't scare me one bit. It's just another police organization—made up of a lot of good men, to be sure, but also some bad ones, as you'll find in any police organization. . . . I'm not dealing with the *Sûreté Générale*, however. I'm dealing with Pierre Delacroix, an individual, who has his weaknesses like all men. You don't want the *Sûreté* in this any more than I do."

"You are wrong about that," he said. "This is all police business, and you are interfering with it in an unforgivable way. You will take the consequences."

"However that may be, I don't want Mlle. de Castro to go to the Villa Le Trayas just yet. There is something going on that I must know more about first. When I have found out enough to satisfy me, then she shall go to the villa and I shall go with her. This is a simple and reasonable position I have taken. I am now responsible for her and her safety. I have assumed that responsibility and I take it very seriously. I don't want to fight you, Delacroix. You are no part of my interest here on the Riviera—or I should say that the *Sûreté Générale* is not."

"I can't accept that," he said. "When we have finished this ridiculous gangster melodrama, I shall notify the *Sûreté* to hunt you down and to exterminate you, if necessary. Do we understand each other, Bodine?"

I raised the gun. I said, "Stop the car."

He slowed down. He glanced at me briefly. There was fear in his face for the first time.

I said, "The War is a long way off and people have forgotten so much of it, which is proper. They have forgotten the violence and the brutal killing. And they've forgotten the reputations of those violent men. So I guess I've got to go out and get myself a new reputation."

He pulled over to the side of the road and stopped with a jerk. He said, looking straight ahead, "What is your proposition?"

"I have no proposition, Delacroix. I find I cannot have you at my back. That's the end of it."

"Wait a minute! . . . If I leave you alone—?"

"You won't. Get out of the car."

There was a desperate look on his face and beads of perspiration stood out on his forehead. He didn't move. He seemed incapable of moving.

"I've got plenty of time," I said. "Don't hurry yourself."

Then he started to talk. The words came tumbling out very fast and I had to concentrate to understand him. He said, "I have handled this all wrong. I admit that to you. I have been very badly advised, which I now realize. As you say, these people have forgotten. . . . I have nothing against you. The *Sûreté* has nothing against you. You are not welcome in France, that is the truth, but so long as you behave yourself you will not be molested. I give you my personal assurance that you will not be molested by me or by the *Sûreté*. Is—is that good enough?"

"All right, Delacroix, drive on and let me out when we come to Mlle. de Castro's car. I know I am making a mistake about you, but I figure I can afford just about one mistake. . . . I think you'd better keep away from me, personally."

He said nothing else. He started driving again, going fast. He slowed down when he saw the other Citroën and he pulled up along side. By that time the old-world look was back on his face, accompanied by the cynical smile. He was a fairly solid performer in his field.

9

I TOOK TITA to St. Tropez, after bidding Delacroix adieu on the highway. As we got under way, I asked her, "Do you want to tell me what happened?"

She was very indignant. She said, "You haven't kissed me yet! You get in the car and you start it up and you ask me, 'Do you want to tell me what happened?' Is this the way Americans act?"

I stopped the car and I put my arms around her. I kissed her with all of the enthusiasm I could summon, which was considerable. I had been too worried about her, too worried about Delacroix, to realize fully what I was doing or neglecting to do. Now she brought me back to earth and to the delightful present.

"I apologize," I said. "I don't know what happens to me—I get off into another world. I was worried about you. If I'd guessed wrong and if you hadn't come along with Delacroix, I'd have been sunk."

"Let's not talk about that. . . . Do you know, darling, that I love you?"

"Fine," I said. "Let's get to St. Tropez. We're wasting a lot of time."

"To a hotel?" she asked.

"That's what I had in mind."

"Then I'll tell you what happened. Just as I started out of the room at the Martinez, this M. Delacroix came to the door with two other men. He showed me his *Sûreté* credentials and he told me I was under arrest. He said that I was charged with a violation of the state security law or something like that. He was vague about it, but he was very definite that I was under arrest, and he had the two other policemen to back him up. He told me that we would go to Grasse immediately and that I would be questioned. So I went out with them and when we got near the front door of the hotel I saw you outside. I stopped him and I demanded that he produce a warrant for my arrest or that I would insist upon calling my attorney. That's what we were arguing about when you looked in and saw us. I was afraid that they would arrest you, too. Delacroix had mentioned your name. He knew we were together. I wanted you to see us and to know what was going on. We went to Grasse and Delacroix questioned me in a little room at the prefecture for an hour. His questions were silly. He was talking about all sorts of absurd things, like atomic energy and the defenses on the border at Belfort and two new battleships they are building at Brest. Then he told me he could parole me in the custody of the Baron de Lys, who was a very respected man, if I wished. He said the Baron had been notified of my arrest and had agreed to be responsible for me. I knew he was lying, but what could I do about it? I agreed to go to the villa and he said he would take me. Then you came along. That is what happened to me."

"It figures," I said. "That's the way Delacroix would operate. . . . Maybe we won't have to worry about him any longer, but I'll be much surprised. I think he'll try again."

"I don't know what you're talking about, darling."

"No, I suppose you don't. . . . Do you want to know what happened to me? I rented this car, first of all. Then I went to your apartment and I searched it."

"Searched it? Whatever for?"

"These," I said. I took out the keys, the bank receipt, and the Bank of Algiers note and I handed them to her.

She looked at them curiously, then laughed. "My treasures!" she said.

"Well, aren't they?"

"I don't know what they are any more than you do! They were left to me by my father, during his last illness. He told me he would explain them to me one day, but he died before he did."

"When did your father die?" I asked.

"During the War. In December of 1943."

"He died as the result of an illness?"

"Of course. Why else?"

"That puzzles me—unless. . . . Tell me, does the name Sandor Barodi mean anything to you?"

"You mean the Count Barodi? Of course! He is a very old friend."

"Of your father? In Spain?"

"Yes. He was in the Revolution with us. I was too young to remember—I was only about three when we came to France—but he visited us often. He was like a member of the family. Then when Father died, he bought our old tumbled-down villa—and he gave us twice what it was worth."

"Nice going. Yes, very nice going. Everything seems to fit in. . . . Tell me one other thing, Tita. Does the Count Barodi or the Baron de Lys know that you have these treasures—these two keys and the bank receipt and the Algerian note?"

"Certainly not. Nobody knows about them—only you, now."

"Well, that's something."

"You have asked me a lot of questions, Alex," she said, taking my hand and kissing it. "You started asking me questions the minute you saw me and the only time you haven't was when we were making love or when you were sleeping. . . . . I love you and I trust you, but I am not a dumb little girl. Now I want to know why."

"It's a job I've taken on," I told her. "I am trying to find out about something, and you seem to have a lot of the answers. That's why I came to you in the first place—for information."

"You are a detective?"

"No—not in the ordinary sense. For many years I was the member of an international espionage organization."

"A spy!"

"Well—yes and no. I've done some work that could be called spying. But mostly it was counter-espionage—getting rid of people who were a danger."

"Getting rid of them how?"

"Oh, one way or another. However it was convenient."

"Not killing them!"

"Sometimes—when it was necessary."

"You do not look the type—no, I will take that back. I saw you like that when poor Pépé came into the apartment and you walked up to him. It was in your eyes for a

62

moment. I was frightened. I thought you were going to kill him."

"So did I, for a moment. But that sort of thing takes youth and lightning-fast reflexes."

"You reflex fast enough for me," she said.

"Can you stand another question?" I asked.

"Not now, Alex. We are almost in St. Tropez and I want to compose my mind for other things. . . ."

"Oh? Like what?"

"Like what we'll do when we get to the hotel, silly."

We didn't do anything when we got to the hotel.

I checked Martita into the Sube et Continental which faces the small fishing port and then I left for St. Raphael to keep my appointment with her cousin and to get money. I persuaded her to take the room in her name and leave mine out of it. I told her that she was to stay in the hotel until I returned and under no circumstances was she to go wandering about the town where she could be seen.

"You talk like I am in the spy business too," she said.

"No, it isn't that. Yesterday in your apartment you were afraid that someone would come—this Vico del Oro. You told me he terrified you. But there's more to it than his looks, whether you know it or not. You should be terrified of him and of others, too. I just want to keep you safe."

"Nobody will find me here."

"I hope not."

I got to St. Raphael in about twenty minutes and parked the Citroën a block away from the apartment. The outer courtyard door was locked—apparently a new policy was now in effect—and I had to ring for the *cordon.* The concierge was in her *loge* and she told me that a number of gentlemen were waiting for me in the apartment.

"A number?" I asked. "How many?"

"I would say there are four."

I started up the stairs. I took the last flight very quietly. I opened the door without any noise. I had the Magnum in my hand. I tiptoed down the hall and looked into the living room. Sitting on the divan were Pedro Lomas and a short, plump man with a soup-strainer moustache. Sitting on a chair by the table and facing them was a character right out of the F.B.I. files. He had a venomous face, dark hair, dark skin, dark eyes, and thin, bloodless lips. This was Vico del Oro, the born thief. I remembered him well from *maquis* days. He was obviously successful in his present trade. Everything about him was expensive, from his seventy-dollar custom-made shoes to the seven-carat diamond that flashed on his left hand, with which he was stroking his hair.

There was no fourth man in sight. I had confidence that the concierge could count up to four. I backed carefully into the hall and waited behind the door, which I had left open. I was not too soon. There was the faint, shuffling sound of footsteps coming down the stairs from the flight above. It was a corny trick—leave one man outside and take the enemy from the rear.

The man came to the doorway and paused. He was listening for something—the sound of the fuss I was supposed to be making, probably. He advanced a step into the hall. I had my right hand raised, the Magnum in it. I brought my hand down hard and hit him on the temple with the gun. He slumped to the floor.

I strode into the living room and pointed the gun at Vico. "Hello, Vico," I said. "Long time no see."

He jumped to his feet, his eyes blazing at me. In an instant Pedro was at his side, the long, thin blade in his right hand and the point of it resting on Vico's neck. Pedro said, "I would have done this sooner but I wanted you to be here."

"Thanks," I said. I waved my gun. "This ought to handle it. Take away his armament."

Pedro gave him a fast frisk, then shook his head. "He isn't armed."

"Fine," I said. "See about the gentleman in the hall." Pedro hurried out and I stood looking at my visitor. He had hooded his eyes and he was smiling at me in a superior way. I looked carefully at him for some sign of recognition, but he apparently didn't know me.

"Who are you?" he demanded.

"Alexis Bodine," I said.

He stopped smiling and his eyes bored into mine. Then

he shrugged. He managed to make it an insolent shrug, which isn't easy.

"Who's that down the hall?" I asked.

"That's Ali. Ben Ali."

"An Arab?"

He nodded.

"First Arab I've ever met who can't walk quietly down a stairway. You need a quiet Arab, my friend. . . . What did you come here for?"

"To see you."

"You didn't know I was here."

"Pépé told us you might be."

"And to see Mlle. de Castro?"

"To see Mlle. de Castro."

Pedro came back bearing a Belgian automatic and an embossed dagger which he had taken from the Arab. He reported the latter was sleeping peacefully. "Keep an eye on M. del Oro," I told him. "I'll take care of the money business."

I went over to the little man on the divan and I apologized for keeping him waiting and for the unfortunate contretemps.

"I've enjoyed it," he said unexpectedly. "I like to see men at work when they are efficient about it."

"I am also Randall McCarey," I said. I showed him my passport. "Did you bring the francs?"

He nodded and produced a briefcase from the floor, put it on his lap and opened it. "For a check on an American bank, I will give you a very good rate. Such checks are at a premium."

I wrote the check and he began counting out francs. Vico had resumed his seat. He couldn't keep quiet. He said, "You are Gerber, aren't you?"

The Swiss banker raised his eyes from his counting. "Yes, Anton Gerber."

"The Sûreté knows all about you. They've got a list of your transactions for the past three years," Vico said.

"Why do you tell me?" asked Gerber.

Vico called him some names, including the French equivalent of punk. Gerber was unperturbed. He finished his counting, handed the bills to me, then closed his briefcase.

He got up and shook hands with me, then bowed to Vico. "The *Sûreté* knows about you, too, M. del Oro," he said. Then he departed.

I told Pedro to try to bring the Arab around and to get him out of the flat. "You take a walk, too," I said. "I want to talk to M. del Oro. Come back in half an hour."

We were alone, Vico, the Magnum, and I. I put the gun away and sat on the divan. I said, "Tell your boss that I'm not interested in him or in you or in his operations. Tell him that I want him to leave me alone and that I'll leave him alone."

Vico sneered at me. He sat back in his chair and crossed his legs. "Where's Mlle. de Castro?" he demanded.

"That's another thing," I said. "You leave her alone. She stays out of it. She stays with me."

"The hell she does!"

"You people are tough. In some ways you are as tough as they come, and so naturally you don't believe me when I tell you anything. You don't remember about me when I was in France in 1942. . . . Well, it's unfortunate for you, Vico. You shouldn't have come here—you shouldn't have come within miles of me. I'm going to take you for a ride —a corny American gang invention. I'm going to blow the top of your head off with my Magnum and I'm going to dump your body on the doorstep of the Baron de Lys' villa. Now, do we understand each other?"

He started to laugh, then he thought better of it. After all, he was alone with me and I had the gun. He wasn't holding anything. He looked at me seriously for a moment, then he began to fidget. "You—you're just talking," he said.

I shook my head. "No. Tonight, Vico, you are the pigeon."

He sat there motionless for a moment. "You son of a bitch!" he said. He sprang out of his chair towards me. But he was too far away. He hadn't calculated carefully enough. I had the Magnum in my hand.

"Sit down, Vico," I said. "I don't want to kill you here. It'll mess up the apartment. As soon as Pedro gets back, we'll get going."

He began to shake. He controlled it with a great effort. He said, "I can try to convince the Baron. . . ."

"Convince him of what, Vico?"

"To leave you alone. To leave Martita alone, too."

"It's no good," I said. "I let you go and you get some gun punks and come after me. Maybe even you'll get me, when I'm not looking. If I dump your body at the villa the Baron and his Corsican friends are going to figure that I mean business and they'll be willing to make a deal."

"What kind of a deal? I—I'll make any deal you say."

"You're small potatoes, Vico. You can't make any deals!"

He slumped down in his chair and he stared at the gun. He was a miserable specimen without his confidence and bluster. It would have been much better for mankind if I had meant what I was telling him. He was certainly no use to anyone.

"What do you want?" he asked. "Money?"

"You haven't got enough to buy a Hail Mary, where you're going."

"I can give you a million in dollars!" he exclaimed in desperation.

"That's heavy ransom for a rat. . . . Well, maybe, if you want to talk. Where does the Baron get his dough?"

"What do you mean? He's got *all* the dough!"

"You know better. So do I. Where does he get it?"

He looked down on the floor, his hands in his pockets. He didn't want to talk but he was frightened. He mumbled a name.

"What?" I demanded. "Speak up!" I cocked the Magnum. The sound of the hammer clicking into place was loud in that room.

"Emil Lutjens," he said.

"Lutjens, eh? He still in Morocco?"

"Yes, sometimes. He goes to Monte Carlo a lot now."

"Who else?"

"That's all."

"Your life doesn't mean much to you, does it?"

"I'm telling you the truth!"

"The hell you are. How about Barodi?"

"What Barodi?"

67

"Any Barodi! . . . O.K., I'm finished with you. You just don't want to live."

He looked up at me and his eyes were wet. "It's worth my life to talk about Barodi," he said earnestly.

"It's worth your life not to. Tell me about Sandor Barodi!"

He shook his head and remained silent. I got up and waved the gun at him. "Come on," I said, "we'll go down stairs and wait for Pedro in the car. He'll be along in a minute."

"Wait!" he said. His voice broke with hysteria. He wiped the perspiration from his face with a shaking hand. "Barodi gives him money," he said finally. "Everything belongs to Barodi—the villa, the banks, everything. The Baron just runs them for him."

"And Lutjens?"

"Barodi owns Lutjens, too."

"And you."

"Yes, and me."

"He'd give a million dollars ransom for you?"

"Oh, I have money of my own."

"O.K. Who killed Pete Dumbrowsky?"

He looked up at me suddenly, his eyebrows raised in surprise. "Pete wasn't killed," he said. "He fell."

The weakness of this method of operation is that you've got to carry it to its bloody end or you're in trouble. You can't let a Vico del Oro run around loose after you've threatened him, any more than you can a Pierre Delacroix. These people come from the toughest school of all and a life means no more to them than any wiggling organic structure they may step upon.

They will never forgive you for an affront. There is no question I had affronted Vico in the only serious way he knew. It would be a blood-feud as long as he remained alive. With Delacroix, it was possibly different. He was more civilized and so he would not act on impulse and emotion. But either way, I was not in a very good position.

10

I WAS LYING on the bed in the room at the Hotel Sube et Continental in St. Tropez, watching Tita get dressed. We were going out to dinner at Les Mouscardins, which is on the *quai* near the hotel. We hadn't left the room for two days—since I had returned from St. Raphael Friday night—and I had had plenty of time to think things out and to do a lot of speculating.

I had thought about what I was going to do about Tita and the Baron de Lys and about how to handle Vico del Oro the next time I met him—which undoubtedly would be a critical personal problem if he got the drop on me. I thought a lot about Pete Dumbrowsky and where and how he could possibly have fitted into this crazy pattern of intrigue and high finance.

This led to the speculation about Sandor Barodi, who now called himself a count, and I wondered who he was and who he had been. Bureau-X had wanted me to identify him, they had said. If an identification was needed, then he was also someone other than Barodi. But the rub there was that I had known a Sandor Barodi, and although my memory of him was dim to the point of uselessness, there was one thing about him I was becoming more certain of the longer I thought about him and the deeper my probings went into my memory. That was that Sandor Barodi was Sandor Barodi and no one else. And yet—there was something about that name that had a special significance, too, and I was certain that it had to do with identity. But what?

Perhaps when I saw him it would come back to me. That was my only hope. For now, there was nothing left but speculation. Well, if he wasn't Barodi—if someone else had taken Barodi's name—and if this was someone I would know, then that would narrow the field a little.

It would have to be someone for whom the circumstances

would fit. Many of the circumstances were known to me—someone who could have been in Spain in 1936; who could have been in Grasse in 1942 and thereafter; who could have been accepted as a friend by the Spanish Minister de Castro and as a confidant by Julo Arbori; who had the imagination and the genius to acquire all of the wealth and the power from a national treasury; who could live openly in France under this name and be accepted by the government and the *Sûreté*. . . . The first name that occurred to me was Komanev, once the private secretary and bodyguard to Stalin, who had known more of the secrets of the Soviet power-plays than any man. Komanev had vanished from the Russian scene in the early Thirties. He was a particularly good prospect because he had been in Grasse in 1942.

Another one was a fellow-conspirator of Komanev who disappeared from Moscow about the same time. He was from Stalin's native Georgia and his true name had never been known to me. He had gone under the name of Vassily Bardov; he had been in Grasse at the right time and also, as I remembered very dimly, he had talked of having been in Spain. But this Vassily Bardov was a real phantom—I had no notion of what he looked like, as I thought about him. The only thing I seemed to be sure of was that there had been a great deal of confusion about him. What kind of confusion I couldn't say.

Either one of those could have done for Barodi, as well as the Roumanian Lorescou, who had fled Russia after killing Mme. Dorelle of the People's Ballet in a drunken brawl at the Metropole. . . . But the more I thought about it, the more names came to me, so all I got out of that thinking was a headache. There were altogether too many people who had been around Grasse and whom I had encountered there for me to begin to catalogue them for this role of Barodi.

Now the important thing, it seemed to me, about this whole affair of Bureau-X and Pete Dumbrowsky was that they had not been primarily interested in the villa of Baron de Lys and its occupants. That was a sideline in their preoccupation, as was the entire matter of the Spanish Republican gold shipment and the discrepancies. Colonel Updyke certainly would not have spoken so frankly about it otherwise, nor would he have expressed so little interest in what was going on at Le Trayas. However, since I had no other leads to follow, and since Martita was apparently in a critical position with these people, I would have to concentrate on that for the time being. One thing at a time. You never know what you are going to uncover. Tomorrow would be Monday and we could go to the Hyères offices of the *Credit Paris-Sud* and find out what was there. That would be another beginning. Maybe.

Martita was putting on her gray Dior suit which I had got to know very well and she was saying, "If I don't get some new clothes pretty soon, I'm going to have to learn weaving. This is about ready to come apart. . . ."

There was a knock on the door—three raps, then two. I got up and opened it and Pedro came in. He said, "They're beginning to gather around the *quai.*"

"Who?" asked Tita.

"The people from the villa," he replied. "I counted four of them."

"Vico in evidence?" I asked.

"I was talking to Bébé Laroche, one who watches the hotel. He said Vico went to Corsica."

"He's got to get his self-respect back. He'll shoot a couple of Corsicians, then he'll come hunting for me. Sit down," I told him. "Rest awhile."

"No," said Tita, "get out. I'm dressing."

Pedro paused with his hand on the doorknob. "What do you think we'd better do?" he asked.

"Nothing," I said. "When faced with the inevitable, relax. They were bound to find us; they've got a good organization. I'm surprised it took them this long."

Pedro left. Tita came over and put her arms around me. "I'm worried," she said. "What will they do?"

"Try to persuade us to go to the villa," I said. "There's nothing to worry about. I think I know, now, how I can handle this."

"How, darling?"

"We'll go to the villa, that's all, and I will talk to this Baron de Lys—tell him what he wants to know."

71

"I don't want to go back there!" she exclaimed. "Alex, I'm afraid. . . ."

"Don't be, Tita. We'll handle this together. You've got to trust me."

She buried her head on my shoulder and held me tightly. I picked her up and carried her to the bed and lay down with her and put my arms around her. "As long as Vico is not there, you've got nothing to worry about."

She snuggled against me. I kissed her warm, soft lips and it was all very protective and close and we were together in a world of our own without menaces and alarums. . . . Then quite suddenly it was something else, as it always was with Tita, and I whispered in her ear, "Let's make love a little. . . ."

She jumped up from the bed and stood regarding me. "Absolutely no!" she said. "I know you, Alex! Along about ten o'clock you'll say it is too late to go out, and you'll phone down for some cold meat and stale bread. No! I insist upon being fed, and properly. It's Les Mouscardins or nothing! I'll—I'll get a divorce!"

So we went to the famous restaurant and we had *langouste grillée* and *chapon farci* and an excellent Montrachet and over the demitasse Tita said, "It was good, all right, but I guess I would have liked it better if we had just stayed in the hotel and had—well, you know, cold meat and stale bread."

Women! How can you figure 'em?

The man came up to us in the foyer of the restaurant and he spoke to Tita. "Good evening, Mlle. de Castro," he said. He bowed to me.

"Good evening, Louis," she said. She introduced him, "M. Padronne, I would like you to meet M. McCarey."

We shook hands and mumbled "charmed" and then he said to Tita, "We have missed you at the villa, mademoiselle. The Baron has asked me to extend an invitation to you, and of course to M. McCarey, to be his guests for the evening."

"I think not, this evening," said Tita. "We have another engagement."

"That is a shame," he replied. "Perhaps another time? Tomorrow evening?"

"Tomorrow evening will be fine," I said, taking Tita's arm and holding her tightly. "We will be happy to call upon the Baron at, say, nine-thirty."

"A most convenient hour," said Padronne. "We shall send a car for you."

"Don't trouble," I said. "We will use our own."

He bowed, kissed Tita's hand, shook hands with me, and was off. Tita took my hand and held it tightly and we left the restaurant and walked along the *quai*.

"I guess it's all right," she said. "When I'm with you I feel safe. . . . Yes, I'll just have to trust you. I've never known a man I could trust, beside my father, and not so long ago I swore I'd never trust a man as long as I lived."

"When was that, Tita?"

"When the Baron gave Vico del Oro the key to my apartment at the villa."

The next morning Pedro had breakfast with us in the hotel room. He reported that the types from the villa were still in evidence. "They are keeping a close watch on the hotel," he said.

Tita shivered. "I don't like it," she said. "Why do they do that?"

"It's normal," I said. "They want to make sure we don't fly the coop. . . . However, some time today we must fly the coop. We've got to get away from them."

"You mean we are going to leave—that we are not going to the villa tonight?" she asked.

"No, just for a few hours. I want you all to myself and I don't want anyone to know about it."

"Phui. You and your plotting!"

"I've done all right so far. We're still alive."

Pedro and I discussed the problem at length, with occasional remarks from Tita. There was no easy solution. There was no rear entrance to the hotel, for one thing. One man at the front door could see anyone who arrived or left. There were a lot of narrow, winding streets at the old fishing port and in the older parts of the town, but they could solve nothing. We had to use a car where we were going, and we couldn't take a car through those narrow byways.

"How about a boat?" asked Pedro.

"A boat to where?"

73

"You and Tita could go on a fishing trip. I'll drive the car around to Ste. Maxime and pick you up there."

"We'll try it," I said. "Arrange to charter a boat for us and order food and wine put aboard. Tell them we'll be out all day."

"I hate boats," said Tita. "Besides, I have no clothes for such an expedition."

I gave Pedro a handful of francs. "Get Tita a heavy skirt and warm jacket," I told him. "Also, flat-heeled shoes. Get me a windbreaker, too. Come on, boy, out with you. Time is of the essence."

Pedro was back by ten with his purchases and a report on the charter. He had obtained a cabin cruiser for us, one that was very popular with the English tourists in the summer, he was assured. Also he had obtained it at the bargain rate of six thousand francs for the day, food and wine *compris*.

"Bargain!" scoffed Tita. "You can buy a boat for that much!"

"It's at the *quai* just opposite the restaurant where you ate last night," he said. "It's painted blue—*le Bouc*."

Tita laughed. "That's appropriate enough for you," she said, poking me with a finger. "The goat! Ha!"

Pedro left to go to Ste. Maxime and Tita tried on his purchases. She was scornful of the shoes, although they looked very good on her small feet, and the skirt, she said, was impossible. But she fixed it so it would hang properly with some pins. She liked a bright red wool shirt and the dark blue jacket, so all was not lost. Not more than fifty per cent.

We were on the *quai* within half an hour strolling arm in arm towards our vessel. One of the villa men followed us at a polite distance. Two others were farther off but not too far. "Do you recognize any of these types?" I asked Tita.

She shook her head. "These are not of the house staff," she replied.

"Pedro seems to know them all," I said.

"He spent a long time there with M. Campo," she said. "He got about more than I did."

We found our boat as advertised. The skipper, a hard-handed native in his fifties, was standing in the cockpit waiting for us. Apparently Pedro had described us for he waved a welcoming hand. Tita said, *"le bouc,"* laughed, and pointed to me. The skipper said gravely, "Welcome aboard. I am Pierre." He spoke very good English.

He asked us whether we would like to fish in the bay or go outside. "There is a stiff breeze blowing today and it will be a bit rough," he said.

"Madame is an excellent sailor," I replied, "so we may as well go outside."

Tita shook her head violently at me and I grinned at her. "That's for *le bouc*," I said.

Pierre started the engine and I cast off the stern lines. Tita and I stood in the stern, her arm around me, as we passed the scores of boats in the small harbor. Then we rounded the breakwater and the *le Bouc* began to bounce. Tita held on for a moment, then turned a stricken face to me. "I've got to lie down," she said.

I helped her to the cabin and stretched her out on the settee. She insisted I stay with her and I sat so that she could put her head in my lap. She said, "This is very comfortable. Now if I could only die. . . ."

I sat there with Tita for about twenty minutes, then went up to the bridge. I asked Pierre, "Can you land us at the dock at Ste. Maxime?"

"Is there something wrong, monsieur?"

"Madame is ill—you know women! Yes, put us ashore at Ste. Maxime and if she feels better we will resume our trip later."

Then he said, "You do not recognize me, monsieur? You do not remember Avril? Pierre Dohaine?"

I looked at him closely for the first time and suddenly a dozen years were shed and I was back at the mayor's house at Grasse and among the famous—or infamous—Fox Group that we had organized when the *maquis* and the F.F.I. had turned itself over to the Communists. . . . *"Quelle date?"* I said.

"Vingt-trois. Et vous?"

"Janvier."

"La date, monsieur!"

"Pour janvier, c'est la quatrieme."

75

We embraced, then, in the manner of the French, and he said, "You have not changed much, my friend. I recognized you the moment you came aboard."

"But you said nothing!"

"I feared it would not be discreet."

"You have grown much older, Avril. . . . And now I remember that you always spoke of boats—that you said some day you would have a great boat of your own."

"Well—this is not a great boat, perhaps, but it does belong to me. . . . Are you still in the espionage business, M. Janvier?"

I laughed. "Only as an amateur now. I'm sort of free lancing. Private enterprise."

"Can we help you?" he asked seriously.

"Who is 'we,' Avril?"

"Group Fox. We are still together. Oh, we are not active as in the old days—mostly we gather to eat and to drink and to tell our lies about the War. Occasionally we help the *pompiers* and just last spring we put out a fire on the Boudreau farm; another time—this was during the winter —we helped to capture a madman who had escaped from the institution at Toulon."

"It is always good to have friends, and even better to find them again after all of these years. I will let you know."

"Fevrier is at the *sous-préfecture* at Grasse and you can always get him by phone."

"Fevrier and his hay fever and his girls!" Aristide Bernard was the one we had called Fevrier because there was always such a windiness about him, like the Levanters.

Avril Pierre Dohaine laughed. "He has not changed, M. Bodine. Only last month there was this widow at Mougins who made serious charges against him in connection with her fifteen-year-old daughter. It turned out that he had been sleeping with the widow for the past six months and that the daughter was incensed because Aristide would not take her to bed when the mother left for work in the early morning at the local *tabac*, and so she told her mother all of the lies about him. . . . You know, Janvier, it takes a genius of a man to get himself so involved with two women—mother and daughter!"

"What was the matter with the daughter?" I asked. "Was she so ugly?"

"Oh no, it was not that. It was that the widow was so demanding and so active that, at his age, Aristide just did not have the stamina for the young one."

"Perhaps we're all too old, Pierre. Perhaps we all belong by a fireside with our slippers and our pipes, instead of aping these young bucks and running about after women and evil men."

"You have found yourself a most charming young companion," he replied, nodding below. "Don't let it depress you."

11

PIERRE TOOK US to Ste. Maxime and went alongside the small dock there. He helped me get Tita ashore. The minute she got off the boat she began to feel better.

Pedro was waiting for us at the dock and I asked him if he wanted to go fishing for the rest of the day.

"Why not?" he said.

"O.K. Be back in St. Tropez by five. We'll meet you at the hotel."

I told Pierre that Pedro was my associate and I knew they would have at least two subjects to talk about, Tita and me.

Martita had been walking around taking deep breaths and the color was back in her cheeks. She came to me and took my arm and we walked to the foot of the pier where the Citroën was parked. On the way she mentioned *le bouc* twice, and I began to fear that I would be *le bouc* from then on. She wasn't going to forgive me for the boat trip.

I drove directly to Hyères, making it in about forty-five minutes, and parked in front of the *Credit Paris-Sud* offices.

"What do we do here?" she asked.

77

"You take these keys," I said, handing her the two I had retrieved from her apartment, "and you go into the man there and tell him you want to open your safe deposit box. See, its number is 568. You then take out whatever is in the box and you bring it out to me. I'll be waiting."

She sat looking at me, saying nothing.

"What's the matter, Tita?"

"These were the keys of my father. . . . I don't know that I have a right. . . ."

"Let me tell you why I am asking you to do this," I said. "Your life may be in danger because it is believed that you have access to the only existing records of Spanish Republican Treasury transactions. These records were in your father's possession before he died, and since you are his only heir it is presumed that you now have them. It is feared that the persons involved in these transactions are prepared to kill you to get the records, or to prevent their being revealed."

"Alex! Are you trying to frighten me?"

"No, darling, I am telling you the truth. . . . This is one of the things I have been concerned with. It's not the primary thing—that's Pete Dumbrowsky. But right now I'm just as interested in keeping you alive as I am in finding out who killed Pete. And anyway, maybe one thing will lead to the other."

"I can't believe it! My father would not have tolerated anything fraudulent!"

"There is no suspicion against your father," I said. "If all of this I am telling you is true, then the worst that can be said of him is that he was the victim of a gang of thieves."

She sat there and thought, shaking her head slowly. Then suddenly she smiled at me and put her hand on my arm. "I said I was going to trust you and I do. . . . All right, let's see what's in the box."

She got out of the car and hurried into the bank. She was gone ten minutes, then came running out. She came up to the window of the car and put her head in. "We owe twelve years' rent on the box," she said. "They won't open it until I pay up. Thirteen thousand, five hundred francs, with taxes, stamps, and the notary fee. I haven't got that much."

I gave her two ten-thousand-franc notes and she hurried off again. Another ten minutes passed. She came out of the bank with a fat manila envelope in her hand. She got into the car, slammed the door, and said, "Let's go. I'm nervous."

I made a U-turn against the advice of signs along the street and started back to St. Tropez. I said, "Open it up, Tita."

She was looking at the envelope and its dozen wax seals as though it had some magic fascination. She read the name written precisely on its face, " 'Martita de Castro.' ... My father wrote that. Then he sealed it up and he put it in that box—twelve years ago! Well, here goes!" She broke the seals and she tore the flap loose. Then slowly she pulled out a letter of a half a dozen pages, written on heavy, embossed paper.

I pulled over to the side of the road and stopped. I said, "You read it, Tita. If there's anything in it that we should both know, tell me."

She nodded her head and began reading. She read slowly and turned each page down in her lap as she finished it. When she got to the bottom of the last page, she picked them all up and handed them to me.

"I guess you were right about a lot of things," she said. Her face was expressionless—almost as though she were in shock.

I looked at the first page. The letter was in Spanish in a small, neat hand and, so far as I was concerned, almost undecipherable. I read the salutation, "My dearest little daughter—" and I handed the sheets back to her. "Read it to me," I said. "Or better yet, translate it as you go—either into English or French. I doubt I would be up to a letter by an educated Spaniard."

She nodded her head and took the letter. I started the car and drove slowly. She read, translated into English: "My dearest little daughter, when you read this I shall have been gone to my final rest, gone from my loved ones and from this material world. As to where, I will not speculate, for I have lived a life that has been both good and

79

bad, in the manner of men. I write this to you, my darling, so as to inform you of one of the good things I have done, not to seek praise or respect from you but only to reveal the one great secret that has been in my heart. It is something you should know about from a practical standpoint, because it is in a way my last will and testament and it will guarantee that you will be cared for amply for the rest of your life. For your dear mother, as you know, I have made other financial arrangements, which I pray she will consider generous. For you there is this:

"When we left Spain, our cause lost, and made our sad emigration to France, I had in my trust for our fallen government the balance of the gold pesetas in the treasury. This specie had been secreted from the avaricious Russians, who came to help us and then betray us for the gold. You should know, daughter, that of the one billion seven-hundred thirty-four million gold pesetas I turned over to our Russian allies, only one-sixth was returned to us in credits for arms and ammunition, and the rest vanished into the vaults of the Kremlin. But that is ancient history and an ancient wound, now healed by the years, and is no part of what I have to tell you.

. "We brought with us from Spain the hidden balance of this gold, which totaled approximately one billion gold pesetas—a little over 300 tons. This has been the best-kept secret of our talkative world, for there remained only three persons who knew of the existence of the gold and of its transference to France. No written record exists of any transaction involving this gold, and even its origin has been eradicated. And now, since I will be gone, there is only one who survives who knows of it. Our beloved president passed on five years ago, as you know. This last survivor knows where the gold is secreted in our villa and how to obtain it.

"Who owns this wealth? Certainly it is not mine, nor is it any man's. Our government has vanished. Our people are scattered to the winds or dead. I will not see it go into the hands of our enemies. I am its steward and the decision is left to me. I know of only one morally acceptable way to dispose of it. The residue of our treasury shall be given to the Church, to the Sisters of Charity whom you know so well and who seek so sincerely to bring light to this darkened world.

"The Church is timeless but we who pay her homage are granted only a brief moment. And so, for this moment that is your lifetime, you will be given the sole use of these funds so that you may be guarded from the evils of penury —no, my dear, I should say, so that you may gain happiness through your generosity and charity. I know you very well, Tita, and I know of the good that you will do.

"The gentleman who has undertaken to carry out my wishes concurs in every detail with this plan, as did our president. He will have made himself known to you long before you have read this last letter, and so perhaps it serves no purpose except to provide an exercise for an old man's whim. It is also true that I promised this gentleman I would not tell you of this arrangement nor reveal his name, so I ask God to forgive me for keeping but half a promise. Trust this friend of mine, for he will guard you with generous and loving care. Trust him as I have trusted him. Go with God. Your Father."

Tita folded the letter and put it back in the envelope. I continued to drive slowly, thinking about this remarkable document and the great world of speculation that it opened.

"Barodi?" I asked her.

"I expected you to ask that," she said. "Some of the conditions fit."

"There is one condition that fits perfectly," I said. "He bought the villa and tore it down."

"There are two others who seem so much more likely," she said, "and they were both at the villa after Father died and before we sold it. But I don't want to talk about it now, darling. I just want to think about this letter and of my father's writing it and of some of the wonderful things he said. . . . He was a fine man, Alex. You would have loved him."

We drove to the outskirts of St. Tropez in silence. Then she said, "There is still another clue. Father was a great reader of mystery stories—he devoured all of the *romans policiers* in three languages—and he loved leaving obscure devices or ciphers lying about to confound me. It was a

81

game he played constantly and I became quite adept at solving his puzzles. Do you think this is why he left me the keys and the receipt from the *Credit Paris-Sud?*"

I nodded.

"And the Algerian banknote," I said. I fished it out of my pocked and handed it to her. "It's all yours, darling. Let me know when you have it solved."

At five-thirty it began to rain, one of those gusty Mediterranean storms that too often make spring on the Riviera so miserable. Tita, Pedro and I were in the hotel room talking over the night's plans and I was doing my best to reassure them both that this visit to the Villa Le Trayas was no danger to any of us.

"They want you at the villa, of course," I told Tita, "and they sent Pépé after you last week, then Delacroix. But if there had been any real crisis they wouldn't have let it go at that. They'd have sent enough men so that your presence would have been assured. . . . From what you have told me, I don't think Vico del Oro's visit was in this connection at all. I think he just wanted to see you and try to make his peace with you—and he brought the Arab along in case I should be there to make trouble. Vico wants you for himself. He's in love with you."

Tita shivered. "What an awful prospect!"

"How about these men they've sent to St. Tropez?" Pedro asked. "Doesn't that mean business?"

"Nothing menacing. They had a crowd out hunting for us and they've concentrated here, now that we've been found. They could have taken us any time in the past couple of days—at least, they could have tried. But they've made no such moves. Instead we were politely invited to visit the Baron."

"So—now what do I do?" asked Pedro.

"You will come with us. You will drive the car and you will wait for us. We will leave for home about midnight, I would say. Maybe before if it gets too dull. You will drive us back to St. Tropez."

"I wish I had your confidence," said Tita.

"You've got to expect people to act according to certain patterns," I told her. "Up to the point of great stress or conflict, they always do. Now Baron de Lys and the rest

82

of them are running a legitimate enterprise. They have unlimited financial backing and all of the power that goes with great wealth. There is not much more out of life that they need. Except for Vico. All he wants right now is you. But otherwise they've got it made. And most important, it is all legitimate. The only police they've got to worry about is Delacroix—and where he fits into this operation is still a mystery to me.

"Under these circumstances it is absurd to presume that they will suddenly become violent and unlawful. They've got too much at stake and they won't jeopardize it by seizing us against our wills or harming us. . . . That will come later, when the pressure is on. That will come when I've pulled their world down about their ears—and all I can hope for is that by then it will be too late for them to do anything about it. . . . The best proof of all of this I can give you is that Vico hasn't retaliated for the way I treated him. Instead of sending a couple of stooges to kill me, he took off for Corsica. Vico is no petunia. He's about as soft as a concrete road at one hundred miles an hour. Sure, he'll try to get his innings—but not now, when all is peace and love and light."

"I'm going to lie down," said Tita. "Too much of this gives me a headache."

"Then I'll go," said Pedro.

"That's a good boy. Be back about ten to nine."

I locked the door after Pedro and Tita said, "Come on over here and talk to me."

"I've been talking to you, honey."

"Yes, but I don't mean that way. . . ."

"I know what you mean. Wait until I make a phone call."

I told the operator to get me the *sous-préfecture* at Grasse and I had to wait only a couple of minutes. I asked the police operator for M. Bernard.

"He is not in his office."

"Can you get him for me? I understood he could always be reached by telephone."

"Who is this?"

"I am a friend. You see, he was supposed to meet this girl and she is with me and she wants him to, ah—"

"Oh, I understand," said the operator. "I'll connect you immediately."

There was a series of clicks, a dead line for a moment, then the voice of Aristide Bernard, unchanged by the years that had passed.

"This is Janvier," I said.

"What? Janvier? . . . Say, who are you?"

"I tell you, Janvier. I am talking to Fevrier, am I not?"

Then he laughed. "My God! Where did you come from?"

"America. I saw Pierre Dohaine today."

"So that is it! You old bandit! Say, when can I see you?"

"Maybe tomorrow, Aristide. That is, if I live through the night."

"My God, it's good to talk to you again! . . . You're not in trouble?"

"No, not yet. But I want you to do me a favor."

"Anything, my friend."

"In your official capacity with the prefecture, can you let it be known to the *Sûreté* that the local police are aware that M. Randall McCarey is going to visit the Villa Le Trayas of the Baron de Lys tonight? Also that he will have with him Mlle. de Castro?"

"Now wait a minute, let me get all of these names straight. This man's name is McCarey?"

"Yes, Randall McCarey. That's me."

"Fine. Glad to meet you, M. McCarey, you old fraud. And this girl's name?"

"De Castro. First name Martita."

"Got it. You'll be at the Villa Le Trayas. You want the *Sûreté* to know."

"To know that the police know. What I'm trying to do is to get the message to Pierre Delacroix."

"Oh—that one!"

"Yes, that one. I want to talk to you about him."

"Any time you say."

"I'll call you."

"Good night, you species of unmentionable."

Tita said, "What was that all about?"

I said, "Do you want to talk about that—or about something else?"

"About something else," she said. "Come on, *bouc*, and lie down here."

12

IN PREPARATION for the visit to Baron de Lys and his
villa full of thugs, I took two guns. The Magnum I put in
my belt and strapped Martita's small automatic on the inside of my upper thigh with adhesive tape. It could not be
seen with my shorts on and it was my fond hope that if I
was stripped—which is always a possibility in this business
—modesty would impel my adversaries to leave me my
shorts at least.

And what about my optimistic and reassuring peroration
to Tita about the peaceful nature of our expedition and
the pattern of non-violence that these people were bound
to follow? Didn't I firmly believe all of that? Well, yes
and no. Mostly no. I was no seer; I had no crystal ball.
There was no way in the world that I could tell whether
my guesses were accurate, whether the expected crisis in
the machinations of de Lys and his crowd had long since
arrived, and whether this was to be the final showdown,
with Tita the ultimate victim and me the sort of side
dish. . . . One may say that it was not intelligent of me
to involve Tita in such a situation, but the truth is that she
had been involved from the beginning, and that it was not
possible for me to protect her if we were apart. While we
were together I would have a fighting chance—even
within the confines of the Baron's domain. But where in
the world could I have left her alone that she would have
been safe?

So we sat close together in the back of the Citroën and
Pedro drove the Corniche to Le Trayas. It was still raining
and blowing and we drove slowly, followed by at least one
of the Baron's cars. Tita poked the Magnum which was
held against my stomach by my belt and she said, "If this
is such a peaceful meeting, why do you bring that?"

"Force of habit," I replied. "I'd feel naked without it."

"You always have a funny answer," she said. "I think

85

it's going to be hilarious living with you—when we get married."

"Who asked you to marry him?"

"Phui! Nobody has to ask! We'll get married when I say so."

"Suppose I've got a wife and six bambinos running around in Virginia?"

"Well—have you?"

"No."

"Then it's settled."

We got to Le Trayas in little over an hour and drove up to the front entrance. It was much more imposing than I had anticipated. "How did it look when you and your family lived here?" I asked Tita.

"It was all cupolas and gingerbread," she replied. "All of this façade is entirely new, and all of the landscaping and the road and the parking area are new. One would not recognize it as our house."

I looked up at the twin towers that were copied from those on the Conciergerie. "The Tour d'Argent is where the royal treasury was kept," I said. "I wonder if there's any significance?"

"Not the way we lived," said Tita. "We were so poor we couldn't keep it heated in the winter."

We were admitted by a butler in white tie into a huge hall, two stories high and hung with excellent tapestries that might have originated at Fontainebleau as far back as François Première. A cute little maid with legs much prettier than one expects in France took Tita's coat. The butler gave me a fast and expert frisk as he helped me out of mine. He didn't spot the Magnum, however, which was right in the center of my belly.

We were escorted to a small study to the right, which Tita told me was de Lys' office. She pointed to double doors opening into the left wing and said, "That is the gaming room. It is a magnificent salon." She held me tightly by the arm but there was no other manifestation of her nervousness.

The Baron was having after-dinner coffee with a handsome, ice-cold blonde whom he introduced as Mme. de Phalle. After the introductions and the hand shakings, we joined them and the blonde poured. She poured with such elegance and she established such a tone of luxurious grace that it was difficult to imagine someone might get shot here within the next hour. . . . Tita relaxed completely.

De Lys said to her, "We have missed you desperately, my dear. Why have you deserted us?"

The Baron de Lys, the former Aldo Arbori of Corsica, had come a long way and the schooling had been effective. He was a small man, not more than five feet seven. In lesser surroundings and in lesser clothes, he would have been no more than another hatchet-faced *maquereau*. In his villa he was the gracious host, the man of the world, the powerful financier who controlled most of the big banks in the casinos of this world's playground. Not only that, but he had a title to back it up and he had a famous beauty to act as his hostess.

Tita said, "I have not deserted you, really. I'm just taking a vacation."

"But you refused to come to see me last week. It was important, Martita. There was important work for you to do."

She smiled at him. She was carrying it off very well. She replied, "I had another engagement, Baron. Didn't Pépé tell you?"

I said, "I'm afraid that was my fault. I wanted Martita to myself."

He looked at me and for a fleeting second his eyes were unveiled for my edification. There was the same concentrated evil that I had seen in the eyes of Vico del Oro and, in the distant past, in those of the Baron's cousin Julo. It is axiomatic, and corny, that the eyes are the windows of the soul. So the Baron had the soul of a glowing cinder which was, I suppose, waiting around to set me on fire. Well, he could hurt you. He had the means and the impulse. He said, "M. Delacroix tells me that you were with the *maquis* during the War."

"That's right," I said. "I went under another name then."

"I had a cousin with the *maquis*," he continued.

"I know. Julo Arbori. Julo got himself killed. He was too greedy."

87

"This War talk is awfully dull," said Mme. de Phalle. "I strongly urge that we select a more appropriate subject."

"A subject more appropriate to this charming gathering," I said. "How about literature—someone like Mickey Spillane?"

Mme. de Phalle laughed and that took off some of the pressure. Baron de Lys smiled thinly and spread his hands on the leather top of his *directoire* desk. He said, "I should very much like to talk to Mlle. de Castro alone, if I may be permitted."

Mme. de Phalle got up and said, "I'll be in the gaming room." She turned to me. "Why don't you join me, M. McCarey?"

"I would rather have M. McCarey remain with me," said Tita. "There is nothing of the business I have with Baron de Lys that he does not know about."

The Baron said, "As you wish, my dear." Mme. de Phalle left the room, closing the door behind her, and I sat back down. De Lys leaned back in his chair and put his hands behind his head. His belly protruded—much more than mine—and he had the definite beginnings of a double chin. He nodded to Martita. He said, "I must try to persuade you to rejoin us here. Various members of my syndicate insist that we continue with your services and they have asked me to offer you a substantial increase. I am authorized to offer you five hundred thousand francs per month and all expenses. . . . And, of course, we would expect you to live at the villa."

Martita shook her head and started to say something. I interrupted. "Mlle. de Castro will consider your offer," I said. "I don't think it is necessary for her to make a decision right now."

De Lys looked at me out of half-closed eyes. "You seem to take a lot upon yourself, M. McCarey."

"I'll tell you why," I said. "Mlle. de Castro is my fiancée and so of course she will not make any commitments that will interfere with our mutual plans. . . . But there is something of possibly greater interest to you that might have a bearing. Earlier today we went to the *Credit Paris-Sud* in Hyères and we opened her father's safe deposit box."

I let it rest there for a moment. The Baron gave no visible reaction. Tita said, "I have had the keys since before he died, but it was M. McCarey who thought it might be important to see what was in the box."

The Baron nodded. "Well?" he said.

"There was nothing in it of any general interest," I said. "The only object there was a personal letter."

"And what could this possibly have to do with my offer?" he asked.

"I'll tell you," I said. "Mlle. de Castro does not have in her possession any of the Spanish Republican Government records of the treasury transactions or any other transactions in which her father was involved. Furthermore, she now knows, from a statement in her father's letter, that these records have been destroyed. I think you should know this before you make any offers to her. I think also that the Count Barodi should be informed of this before he tells you to make any offers to her."

De Lys suddenly sat forward and his eyes bored into mine. He said, "I've heard a lot about you, for years now, and I wouldn't trust you with a *prix unique* rhinestone!" Then he controlled his anger and he put on his most engaging smile for Tita. "Let me at least show you how I've redecorated the apartment for you," he said to her.

She looked at me questioningly. "Why not?" I said. "We'll take a look."

De Lys jumped up and opened the door. He was again the affable lord of the manor. We followed him up the huge stairway to the left of the main hall and he chatted about his plans for doing over the rest of the apartments in the east wing. We followed him down a long hallway, then along another that made a right-angle turn to the left. At the end was the door to the apartment he had prepared for Tita. He opened the door with a key and stood aside for her to enter. I followed her, then turned against the wall to let the Baron go by me. Tita was enchanted with the apartment, as any woman would have been. The walls were done in padded *toile de joie* and the furniture was very beautiful English Sheraton. This Aldo Arbori had come a long way if he had sense enough to select a decorator with such taste.

I, of course, was trying to figure the angle—the why of

89

all this maneuvering. Looking at a new apartment was an innocent enough pastime, but why? Did de Lys think he could entice Martita with this? We sat down in the small living room and he talked to her of mutual friends and acquaintances. He could be charming when he wanted to be and it was easy to understand how he had ingratiated himself with the rich baroness in the first place, which had been the start of all of this fortune.

Then he said to her, "I have redone your old office, if you want to take a look at it."

"Oh, I would love to!" she said. She jumped up and went out. I heard the door close.

The Baron sat there looking at me. Perhaps he was waiting for Tita to come back. Perhaps not. . . . He said, "Delacroix told me who you were. He's a valuable man, Delacoix."

"Yes, I told him to tell you."

I had my right hand on the butt of the Magnum under my coat but I wasn't quick enough. De Lys had a short-barreled .38 pointing at me before I knew it. He said, "All right, Bodine, get up. We'll go down the hall."

I preceded him out of the apartment and down the hall to the turning. He told me to stop there.

What happened was that the door to my left opened and a couple of dark-suited thugs pulled me into the room. The door banged. Something crashed against the back of my skull and that was the end of consciousness.

I came to on a concrete floor. There was the strong smell of carbolic acid in the concrete. A bright light was burning overhead and I opened my eyes slowly. My head and my shirt were wet. I had no coat. Someone said, "He's come around. Let the son of a bitch have it!"

Some men, at least two, went to work on me with feet and fists and there was a stinging across my back that might have been a whip. I didn't stay conscious long.

Then there were several intervals of semi-consciousness and vague voices. Oddly, there wasn't much pain. There was a thumping and a thudding as the blows struck, but I wasn't being hurt. I had a feeling almost of contentment. It seemed that I was floating very lazily through space and that there was violence all around and about me but it didn't touch me.

Then I came to with a sudden start and I was aware of great pain for the first time. My entire body ached like an ulcerated tooth. There was the taste of blood in my mouth and one of my eyes wouldn't function at all. The eye that would looked up at the bright overhead light. I rolled my head over slowly. The same concrete and the same smell.

There was the voice of a man talking. It seemed to be in the far distance and it took several seconds before I could make out the words. I heard, ". . . dump him out on the beach the other side of Cannes. You know that back road down to the gulf? . . . Yes, the doctor said he'd live that long. We don't want him to die around here. We'll give him a shot in the head when we get there."

Another voice said, "Jesus, what a hangover!"

I rested there for several minutes and I thought about that: Jesus, what a hangover! I reached my right hand down to my thigh and felt for Tita's automatic. It was still there. All I had to do was to get it.

It wasn't easy. My hands didn't belong to me at all. They wouldn't do any bidding and I had to watch them and will them powerfully to work for me. Then suddenly I seemed to regain control of them and I got the gun. I didn't even notice any discomfort when I pulled the adhesive away from my skin.

I had the automatic in my right hand and I pushed myself backwards until I came against a wall. Then I pushed myself up into a sitting position. All of this was extremely painful and may have taken as long as half an hour. There were still voices from time to time, but I paid no attention to them. There was no one to be seen in my range of vision.

I sat there for maybe another half hour and I began to feel better in one way. My abrasions and contusions were more painful, but my head was clearer and I had better co-ordination. I felt that I could stand up, if I had to, and could even walk if I could brace myself against a wall. Also I had been able to open my left eye a small crack and I was cheered considerably to know I could see out of it.

Two men appeared from around a wall and came toward me. One said, "The bastard moved! How did he do that?"

The other said, "Maybe we'd better give him some more. He looks too spry."

The first said, "No, we'll move him, like the boss said. You want to beat somebody up, why don't you try me?"

They came toward me and bent down to look at me, standing side by side. I shot each in the head with the small automatic. It seemed to me that there was an hour between the shots, but they must have been very close together because the second man I killed had not moved his head more than a few inches after the first shot.

I found a gun on each. I put the small automatic in my pants pocket and took an American .38 from one of them, a dark-skinned thug who looked like an Arab. It was fully loaded and it was well kept.

I got to my feet and leaned against the wall to rest. I was not dizzy, just tired. Then I moved slowly around the wall, a foot at a time, and out of the room into a hallway. It was obvious that I was in a cellar. To my right was a stairway and I made for that. I sat on the bottom step and rubbed some of my bruises. If I could find some brandy for the inside of me and some water for the outside, I would feel a lot better. I crawled up the steps, not without pain, and stood up at the top with my hand on a door. There were voices on the other side of the door. I could make out no words.

I opened the door with my left hand and I swung into the room with it, holding the gun in my right. It was the kitchen of the villa. Seated at a table directly in front of me, over coffee and brandy, were two men. One was dressed in the white coat and pants of a chef. The other was the butler in his shirt-sleeves.

I said to the butler, "Where's the Baron?"

He sat looking at me, his mouth open. I waved the gun at him. I said, "Talk fast, you son of a bitch. It may be the last talking you'll do on this earth."

He began to jitter. He said, "The Baron left hours ago for Antibes."

"To go where?" I demanded. "To see whom?"

"To go to El Dorado, sir. That is the villa of the Count Barodi."

I demanded, "Where's the lady I came with, Mlle. de Castro?"

"She went home, sir."

"When?"

"About half after eleven, sir. Pedro Lomas drove her to St. Tropez."

"That's a lie! They wouldn't have left without me!"

"Oh yes sir! The Baron gave Mlle. de Castro your note."

"My note! . . . ." I felt a sudden wave of nausea and I gripped the door hard to keep from falling. "Pour me a drink of that brandy," I ordered. "Put it on the edge of the table. The two of you get up and stand by the sink facing me."

They did as they were told. I reached for the brandy and drank it in one gulp. I dropped the glass on the floor. The butler made a sudden dive to get out of my gun range behind a steam table in the center of the kitchen. I shot him in the chest and he collapsed on the floor, moaning. I said to the cook, "Don't you do anything foolish."

I sat at the table and poured another brandy. I drank that and I felt much better. I had been ice-cold inside and now that feeling was gone. I looked at the cook, who was shaking like an aspen. He was an elderly little *pederaste* with no stomach for this violence. "I need a car and I need someone to drive it," I told him. "How about you?"

"Yes sir. I can drive."

"Fine. Is there a clothes closet here with a coat in it that will fit me?"

He nodded. "Right there," he said, pointing.

"Open it and show me the coat."

He did as he was told. I motioned him away. I walked easily—that is, relatively easily—to the closet and I put on the coat. It fitted well enough. "O.K. Lead the way to an automobile. Don't walk too fast. I want you within close gun range." Then I saw the sink and I remembered that I needed the water outside. "Wait a minute," I said.

He stopped and watched me. I took off the coat and I put the gun on the drainboard within reach. I slopped cold water on my face and head. It felt marvelously soothing. I

93

took my time about it, then dried myself with a couple of dish towels. I put the coat back on. "Get going," I said.

The cook led me down a hall, across a porch, and out the back door. There was a huge garage to the left and he headed for it, me following. He opened a door that went overhead and I saw a Cadillac convertible, a Mercedes Benz 300 S.L., a Daimler town car, and some lesser vehicles down the line. I pointed to the Cadillac. "We'll use that," I said. "Stand right there until I get in. Then come to the side slowly and seat yourself."

He was co-operative. He started the engine and we were off, along the driveway that curved around the villa and down to the Corniche. "Turn right," I told him. "Get to St. Tropez as fast as you can make it."

The rain had stopped, the road was dry, and we pulled up in front of the Sube et Continental in half an hour. I told the cook, "Go back to the villa and put the car away. Then call the police. Tell them you don't know what happened—that you were in bed and you heard some shots. I'm letting you go because you look as though you had some sense. Otherwise I'd kill you too. Do you understand?"

"Yes sir," he said.

I went up to Tita's room and knocked on the door. She opened it almost immediately. The minute light in the hall had gone off and she could not see me clearly. I said, "Darling, I—"

Then I collapsed in her arms.

13

Seldom has there been experienced along the Riviera an uproar such as that which followed what the press called the "Massacre at the Villa Le Trayas." The finding of the three bodies—the butler too was dead when the police responded to the cook's call—and the evidence that a fourth man, obviously a blood-thirsty assassin, had somehow vanished completely after his foul deeds, made the most sensational reading.

I woke up about noon and Tita was sitting beside the bed with a cup of coffee in her hands. I had been cleaned up and salved and bandaged. I ached all over. I felt as though I had just taken a trip through a meat grinder. I said, "Good morning, sweetheart. Did you get the license number of the juggernaut?"

She shook her head at me and pursed her lips. "Drink this," she said. "You don't have to try to be funny just now."

I drank the coffee. It was bitter and hot and it hurt all the way down. Then she handed me a note written in ink on the Baron de Lys' stationery. I read it slowly out of my good eye: "Darling—Go back to St. Tropez with Pedro. I must talk to the Baron about a very important matter and I must go with him to Nice. I will see you in the morning. Love. Alex."

"Didn't you write that?" she asked.

"No. It's not mine. It's not my style. You've never seen my handwriting, have you? One day I'll write you a note. . . ."

"All right," she said, "that clears up that. Now do you want to tell me what happened?"

"No, darling, no details. They wanted to hurt me and they did. I shot my way out. That's all there is to tell."

She produced a copy of the final edition of a Paris morning newspaper. She read a brief dispatch on page one—a sort of preface to the hundreds of thousands of words that were to follow giving all the lurid details of the massacre, the opinions of the police and any others who had them, and the intimate histories of all those connected with the villa. "A most violent and revolting crime took place at Le Trayas, villa of the Baron de Lys, early today," she read. "Three of the Baron's household were shot down in cold blood as they went about their early-morning duties. The blood-thirsty assassin slew two of his victims in the cellar of the villa, and then went to the kitchen and shot down the butler, a M. Duval, said to be from Arles. The names of the other two victims were not immediately learned. The police are investigating and they report that the assassin made good his escape, probably by automobile. Road-blocks have been set up around the entire area and an early arrest is expected, according to Inspector Jordain. 'This madman will not evade us,' the Inspector told a reporter. 'We will have him in our hands before the day is out.' "

"Sketchy," I said, "but certainly not inaccurate. The facts are there."

"Listen, blood-thirsty assassin, how long do you think it's going to take the police to find you? Do you think you came into this hotel last night, all cut up and bleeding like a stuck pig, without anyone noticing you? Do you think the Baron is going to keep quiet about you? Do you think no one else observed you?"

"The answer to all of your questions is yes and no," I said. "However, we do have one weak link—the cook. Will you please get M. Aristide Bernard on the phone for me? You will find him at the *sous-préfecture* at Grasse."

The connection was made quickly and I heard Bernard's cheery greeting. "Where are you?" he asked. "We want to see you."

"Sube et Continental in St. Tropez," I said. "Room 301. It's not in my name."

"Of course. Avril and Juin will call on you. They are standing by."

I hung up and I tried to smile at Tita. Maybe I shouldn't have. She looked horrified. "Rest your fears, little dove," I said. "The Marines have landed and the situation is in hand."

She shook her head. "In my opinion," she said, "we are now in the soup. . . . Well, you had to go to the villa. You just had to!"

"Are you second-guessing, Tita? Don't feel bad about anything that happened. It's all part of the job. It was bound to happen to me. I asked for it. I provoked it. They had to make a try for me, and if I could survive I could beat them. It's always that way, darling, in this business. It's just a normal risk—the same sort of risk a bookkeeper takes, that he will cut his finger sharpening a pencil. . . . I admit that I was a lot closer to my demise than I had intended. But I'm not as spry as I used to be and I miscalculated the period of unconsciousness. However, it has all turned out well so far. Now I have them on the run. You will see; from here on in we will have an hysterical disorganized group to deal with. I can now pick them off one by one at my leisure. I can settle your problem and I can find the man who killed Pete Dumbrowsky. They are afraid and you will see how such people act when they are impelled by fear."

"You talk big," she said, getting me a cigarette and lighting it, then putting it in my sore mouth. "But I guess I can stand this big talk if you can. . . ."

Pierre Dohaine—Avril—arrived in a few minutes with a man I had completely forgotten. Juin was a heavy-set, stolid, and taciturn type named Sebastien Luchon and he was now a sergeant in the *gendarmerie*. Tita nearly flipped when she opened the door and saw his uniform. I think that if she had had her gun, she would have started immediately to shoot her way out. But her fears were quickly calmed when Luchon came to the bed and embraced me like a brother.

"Alex, my old friend!" he exclaimed. "Flat on your back with cuts and abrasions! It is surely like old times!"

Tita got them chairs and they sat looking at me, shaking their heads. Dohaine said, "You telephoned Bernard last night and you told him that you and Mlle. de Castro would be at the villa. So the *gendarmerie* and the *Sûreté* know that you were there."

"I had to do that," I said. "I had to protect Martita. I knew they would not try for both of us together under such circumstances. Well, it was me they wanted first, so it worked out."

"What is your story?" asked Luchon.

"Mlle. de Castro and I left the villa together about eleven-thirty. Pedro Lomas will testify to that, and so will Mlle. de Castro, of course. . . . I was injured falling down stairs. Drunk, you know."

Dohaine laughed. Luchon gave me a sour look. Tita sat on the edge of the bed and told me I was talking too much. She was probably right, in whatever way she meant it.

"It's a bad business," said Luchon, shaking his head.

97

"We will never hear the last of this. Such a massacre hasn't taken place in France since the war. We are bound to catch the culprit, if it takes the life of every man on the force. . . . Do you know what the orders are, my friend? All leaves are cancelled; the platoon system is in the ashcan and we work as many hours as the slave-drivers who direct us have a mind to demand. We are to carry our arms at all times, even to bed with us, and that can be a mighty nuisance, I can tell you. We lose all of our privileges until this murderer is behind bars—even that of our coffee in the guardroom. . . . Tell me this, Alex, where did you get the gun?"

"I had it strapped to my leg," I said. "Fortunately they didn't find it when they searched me."

"An old trick, but the old tricks are the best. And what if they had found it?"

"Their plan was to dump me on the beach east of Cannes—on the gulf. I would be found shot in the head."

"That is what Group Fox wanted to see you about," he said. "We had to know these details. . . . I did not know until this morning that you were back in France. Late last night when I read the first bulletin on the teletype about the massacre at the villa, I said to the lieutenant, 'I wonder if this Alex Bodine has come back to the Riviera.' Those were my very words, believe me!"

"All right," I said, "now this is what I need from Fox Group. The cook at the villa, who drove me to the hotel, is the weak link. He won't stick to his story if there is any pressure. He is a little *pederaste* about fifty with the guts of a shy chicken. He is the only witness and the only one alive who can place me at the villa at the time of the shootings. Can you take care of him for me?"

"Of a certainty," said Dohaine. "We will remove him to a safe place immediately."

Luchon nodded in agreement. "Was there anything else?" he asked.

"I'd like to know the movements of the Baron de Lys and of this other Corsican type, Vico del Oro. It's not too important but it would be interesting and it would give Fox Group some practice."

"I don't need any practice," said Luchon. "That's all I get on this job."

"Well, the others, then. . . . Also, I'd like to know what goes on at the Hotel Nouvel in St. Raphael and where Count Barodi fits into that picture. . . . The Count is Sandor Barodi who was with Julo Arbori at Grasse in the Forties. Now he's got nothing but money and he's doing something with it that is connected with the Hotel Nouvel. That's my guess. A friend of mine, Pete Dumbrowsky, lost his life trying to find out."

"I remember that case," said Luchon. "Inspector Jordain and Delacroix of the *Sûreté* said it was suicide or accident. I never heard it was anything else."

"It was something else," I said. "He was killed. If you happen to find out who killed him, I want him."

They agreed to undertake the investigations, then got up to go. Dohaine pulled a folded newspaper out of his pocket and tossed it to me. "Here's the latest on the crime," he said. "We'll see you in a day or so. Call Bernard if you need us."

They left after effusive adieus and after Luchon, at the door, had told Martita, "As long as he's warm, he's a menace to the whole human race. Run for your life."

"I like them," she said. "They make me feel that we are not alone."

She changed some of my bandages and she used a whole jar of salve on my back, which she told me had been badly cut up. Then she read to me the more complete account of the "Massacre at Le Trayas" in the *Apres-Midi* which Dohaine had left. There were a couple of paragraphs that intrigued me. One said, "The Baron de Lys could not be reached for any comment. It was announced at the villa that he had gone abroad for his health. Later the police confirmed that he had left France. His destination could not be learned."

The other paragraph read, "It was learned from an authoritative source which must remain anonymous that these brutal murders were undoubtedly political in motive and that the perpetrator of these dastardly crimes is the paid agent of a foreign government. It is believed that the murderer was spirited out of France by accomplices within

99

hours of the shootings and that he is now under the safe protection of his native government. It was specifically denied by this source that these murders were in any way connected with the uprisings in North Africa or that any Arabic nation is involved. However, in view of the fact that one of the victims was an Arab, Akbir el Fessal, said to be prominent in the councils of the Arabic League, this avenue of investigation will be continued by the *Sûreté Générale.*"

There was one notion that kept recurring to me ever since I had arrived on the Riviera and had given thought to the geographical position of the Côte d'Azur. That was that this playground in the sun was ideally located as the contact point for two troubled areas of the world. One was the Near East and the other Algiers. And if there was any relationship between the Arab uprisings in Algiers and the Arab mobilizations further east, then the direction of it well could have centered on this French coast. Let me make it clear that this is not the kind of thinking one encounters in the normal and usual activities of everyday life. This is the unique cerebration of the spy-hunter who must approach his problem always from the standpoint of "might be."

There were a number of factors that made this "might be" a greater likelihood, not the least of which was the fact that Bureau-X was active in this area. I would have the jump there on the lay analyst because I knew about Bu-X; I knew what kind of an organization it was and I knew why it functioned. I will concede that the presence of an operator of Pete Dumbrowsky's stature would not prove very much. It was unlikely that he would have been assigned to the more critical and important spots. His work was down on a lower echelon, generally, but that would not have precluded his having stumbled upon something big—too big for him to handle—with the subsequent mobilization of the elite. . . . I liked it that way because there were two things that pointed to it. One was the presence on the Riviera of Colonel Updyke. The other was the refusal of Bureau-X to become interested in Pete's demise.

I was certain that Updyke's quick acceptance of Pete's death as accident or suicide was merely a cover-up. I was certain that he feared any active investigation of it would jeopardize something bigger and more important to him. . . . Well, I didn't work that way. I had never been an admirer of Updyke and his school. I was not a proponent of the subtle and the indirect. I had been taught the point-blank methods of the founders of Bureau-X. I had been brought up on the simple creed that one must first find the enemy, then destroy him.

Now everything from the very beginning of this account has pointed to one man as the probable enemy—Sandor Barodi. One might logically contend, upon the facts that I have given, that it was now necessary only to seek out Barodi, kill him, and solve the whole problem. But you can't go on facts alone. I've presented them all as they were revealed to me and yet, in my opinion, they didn't prove a thing of any real importance. All that they proved was that this Barodi was very wealthy; that he would have all of the power that went with such wealth; that he owned a number of people and at least one huge enterprise; that he had been a close enough associate of the late Don Carlos Ortega de Castro-y-Lomas to have bilked the Spanish Republican Treasury out of hundreds of millions in gold. These facts also would demonstrate that Barodi *could have been* the evil mover in the death of Pete Dumbrowsky and also he *could be* engaged in political machinations with the Arabs and the Russians.

But let us look at the non-facts. They are much more interesting. Non-fact A is that Barodi as an individual never could have gained control of this great wealth and so he was merely representing other persons or groups or a government, even. Non-fact B is that this relationship might be revealed if and when Barodi was identified—in other words, when his origin became known. Non-fact C is that Barodi couldn't have had anything to do with Pete Dumbrowsky's defenestration because he wasn't there or he wasn't interested in it. . . . The final non-fact is that a Monsieur X killed Pete for reasons of his own, which were sufficient for him but had nothing to do with any of the rest of it.

You see what I mean about how interesting non-facts can be?

My convalescence took two weeks. They were the most delightful two weeks of my life, the aches and pains be damned. I was nursed and loved by this Spanish girl who grew more a part of me and more precious to me as each hour passed. And nothing else happened that I cared about or would pay any attention to. Dohaine, Luchon, and finally Bernard of Fox Group visited me and reported various activities of theirs and of the people in whom I was interested. There was nothing worth remembering, outside of the fact that Vico del Oro had been seen at Antibes.

A cousin of Tita's, a medical man by the name of Luis Ortega, came to see me three times. He was a round little man with pince-nez on a black ribbon, white piping on his vest, and a vile temper. On the third visit he said, "What a waste of time! You are healthier than I am. Good-bye!"

On the fifteenth day I got up and I put on a new suit that Tita had ordered made for me by a local tailor by the name of Delahouse who claimed he had learned cutting on Bond Street. Maybe he had, but not Bond Street, London. Bond Street, Bombay, most likely. It fitted like a sack, or sari, and it had some of the most unusual drapes I've ever seen on a male form.

"It's fantastic!" I said. "That man can make a fortune running up tents for the Arabs."

"At least it hides your big belly," Tita commented.

I opened the coat. "I haven't got a big belly any more," I said, and showed her.

"You should be beaten up more often," she said.

"Don't worry, darling. I will be."

14

FIFTEEN DAYS HAD PASSED since the massacre at the Villa Le Trayas and most of the sensationalism of it had worn thin. The *Paris-Soir* that I bought in the hotel lobby had put the story on the back page down among the medicine ads and they told all they had to tell in a niggardly two hundred words. What it amounted to was a report that there was nothing to report. No new arrests, no new suspects, no new avenues of investigation, no new opinions by police or politicians. I walked along the *quai* in my ill-fitting suit and wearing dark glasses to hide the purple discoloration around my eyes. Nobody took any notice of me. I guess in a suit like that, I had finally achieved the native coloration of a St. Tropezite. I strolled around to the head of the *quai* and I spotted Dohaine's boat. He was on the after-deck bent over his work. I stopped above him on the *quai* and watched him take apart his carburetor. He didn't look up at me. He said in a low voice that would not carry much beyond my ear, "A new one showed up here yesterday. He watches every move I make. Now he's connected you with me."

"Where is he?"

"On the café terrace with the fancy redhead. He packs a gun in a shoulder holster. You can't miss him."

"I'll have a look at him." I walked along to the end of the *quai,* then came back towards the boat and the small café called Chez les Matelots. On the terrace was a girl I would have known anywhere—the redhead of the Jaguar and the dirty gesture. Her companion was a stocky, tough-looking man of about my age with features that might have been Slavic. The girl was watching me with frank interest as I approached. The man was reading a newspaper and paying no attention to anyone. There was an empty table just across the aisle from them and I took it. She gave me a tentative smile. The man continued reading.

I ordered a *café noir* and sat there basking in the noon sun. There was no conversation from across the aisle. The man was still reading, the girl looking around for something—anything. I caught her eye and she smiled at me again. Then she got up suddenly and went into the café, probably to go to the ladies' room, but more probably to have me follow her and make a date with her inside. I sat where I was and got a good look at the man. There was no question that he was in the business. Everything about

103

him was immaculate and efficient; his shoes were shined, his nails were polished, and his hat had been recently cleaned. Also he wasn't bored. He was alert, waiting for something.

Presently he turned his head towards me and our eyes met. His remained expressionless. They were a washed-out blue and fish-cold. They held mine for just an instant, then he turned his head slowly and looked back into the café. I got up, paid the waiter who came hurrying from inside, then walked back along the *quai* to the hotel. Up in the room Tita was mending a seam in her skirt and she pointed out to me once more that she would have to have some clothes.

"You'll move back into your apartment in St. Raphael," I said. "You've got three closets full of clothes there."

"I'll move back! And what are you planning to do, my pigeon?"

"I'm not sure. Let me make a phone call first."

I put a call through to Grasse and got Bernard on the second try. The first time around I was told he was not available. They had a new operator on the police switchboard.

"Has Avril told you about the man who came to St. Tropez?" I asked him.

"Yes. We're working on him."

"Why's he staked out on Avril?"

"Your guess is as good as mine. Maybe he was waiting for you to come along."

"What's Avril been doing the past week?"

"He's been in and out of St. Raphael."

"Where's this guy staying?"

"You'd never guess! At the Nouvel! He registered there Tuesday under the name of Ilia Pateck. His passport is Yugoslav and he has a tourist visa good for three months. He speaks French with a good Parisian accent and he knows his way around the Riviera."

"You pick up quite a bit."

"Old Robert Senes got a job as a waiter at the Nouvel. Pastiche died. . . . Maybe you don't remember Robert? He was our first Novembre. He's the one who retired with a bullet in his shoulder. Well, it's all right now."

"O.K. Who's the redhead?"

"What redhead?"

"The one Pateck is with today."

"I haven't caught up with today yet. A redhead, you say? What does she look like?"

"Money. A beautiful girl, dark red hair and green eyes. Couldn't be over twenty-six. Good figure, good legs, and expensive clothes. The first time I saw her she was coming out of the Villa le Trayas in a Jaguar with a blonde."

"Oh!" he exclaimed, "Suzie! She's one of our foremost tourist attractions here on the Riviera. She's actually a nice girl, Alex. Comes from Juan les Pins. Her father's an artist over there, Jean Lautrey. She does a bit of high-level whoring when she gets bored or when she needs new clothes—but who doesn't? No, Suzie is a good girl, although much too expensive for my pocketbook. I remember one time—"

"Listen," I interrupted, "all I want is information. I'm not hunting for girls."

"I forgot. You got yourself all tied up like a pig going to market. Too bad for you."

"Good-bye, Fevrier."

I hung up. I was under the close scrutiny of Tita. She demanded. "What's all this about redheads?"

"Girl down on the *quai*," I said. "She acted as though she wanted to meet me. She was with another guy."

"Now you know her name and where to get hold of her, eh?"

"Oh sure. What is this? You have any doubts about me?"

She laughed then. "I'm just acting like a Spanish girl is supposed to act," she said. "I figured that if I didn't you'd feel cheated."

I took her in my arms. "I haven't been cheated out of a thing, sweetheart," I said.

So pretty soon we were lying down on the bed together, and *subito*—

St. Tropez and the Hotel Sube et Continental had served their purpose. Tita and I went back to her apartment on the rue Honoré-Vadon in St. Raphael that afternoon. Pedro drove us in the Citroën and on the way over I told

Tita, "I think it's about time we made some plans. I think that this business of mine will all come to a head very quickly. All of a sudden one day everything will be solved, and on that day we will want to leave for America. . . . I can't take you with me unless we are married."

She said in a very small voice, "I don't know whether I want to go with you to America." She took my hand and she kissed it and she put it against her cheek. "I've waited an awfully long time for this, and now that it's here I'm afraid."

"There's nothing to be afraid of, Tita. I won't mistreat you more than one would normally expect. I'll beat you no more than once a day. . . . Look, darling, America isn't far. It's twelve hours or so away by plane, that's all. We can come back here as often as you like. You do not have to abandon the world that you know or the kind of a life you like."

"Oh, it isn't that," she said.

"Then what is it?"

"Do you love me?"

"Oh that!" So I told her I loved her in several different languages and that seemed to help. Then I said, "I want you to go to Paris and buy your trousseau. I would like Pedro to go with you. I will get the money today, if I can find Gerber, and I should like you to leave tomorrow."

She nodded her head and she thought about it. But she didn't agree. She said, "So you can get the redhead, eh?"

"My God! I thought you weren't jealous!"

"Well, I'm not. Not one little bit. But if I hear of your having anything to do with that redhead, I'll cut you up in little pieces. Jealous, ha!"

"I have no inclination toward any other woman," I told her. "Neither the inclination nor the strength."

We found the apartment at No. 8 airless and dusty. Tita went to work immediately to get it back to its former immaculate state and Pedro went off to find Anton Gerber. I went out for a walk. I had to find out whether Ilia Pateck was after me, or whether he was going to be satisfied with Dohaine and other members of the Fox Group.

I knew I was dealing with a professional. One look at him had told me that. Also, there had been no sign of him

106

since I had seen him at the café. Dohaine would have known whether he had followed me from St. Tropez, but there was no way to reach the boatman by phone. Certainly I would have known tomorrow when Dohaine made his report to Bernard, but it was always possible that tomorrow would be too late. One never waited for tomorrow.

I walked purposefully past the Hotel Nouvel to the boulevard, turned right and strode to the place Casino, then right again along the boulevard Felix Martin. I turned on the rue Admiral Baux towards the railroad station. Up to that point no Pateck or no redheaded Suzie. I went to the station and bought two first class tickets to Paris for tomorrow morning's express.

I had plenty of opportunity to look around and I could have taken an oath that Pateck was not in the station. There was one way to make sure. The gates were open and people were boarding a local to Nice. I strode to the gate. I gave the guard one hundred francs in lieu of a platform ticket and explained that I was rushing to see a friend off. He passed me through and I hurried along to the first-class carriage at the front end of the train and got into an empty compartment. In five minutes the guards yelled their warning, the whistle blew and the train started. French trains accelerate fast and you don't waste time. I had the door open and was off before it had gone fifty feet.

I turned quickly as I hit the platform and faced the rear of the train. A man from one of the rear coaches jumped to the platform only seconds after me. I couldn't see his face from that distance, but it was Pateck all right. The hat and the suit certainly were his. There is no question about it, he was good.

With Tita and Pedro in Paris, I spent the next couple of days sitting in the chair Pete Dumbrowsky must have occupied hundreds of times, studying the Hotel Nouvel across the courtyard as he must have done. However, there was one major difference in Pete's activity and in mine; I didn't have the least notion what I was hunting for. Pete knew something that I didn't and so I was just wasting time. But I didn't have anything else to do and there was always the thousand-to-one chance that I would.

107

see someone or something in the hotel that would help me to piece this puzzle together.

Also, if I didn't leave the apartment I wouldn't be followed by Pateck. I'd had enough of that gumshoe.

On Friday I got a call from Bernard and he was bubbling over with his news. He had been in Cannes the day before and he had run into redheaded Suzanne Lautrey at the Palm Beach Casino, where he'd gone on police business. "I do the collecting each month," he said simply. "I get ten percent for this trouble."

"To hell with that. What about Suzie?"

"I was getting to her. I asked her what she was doing with this fellow Pateck and she said she met him in Antibes. I said, 'What were you doing in Antibes?' She said, 'I was at a party.' I said, 'Whose party?' She said, 'None of your business.' So there it stands. But Barodi's villa is in Antibes and he knows her very well—they had quite a thing going a couple of years ago. Anyway, then came the chopper. She asked me about you! She said, 'Who is this American who calls himself McCarey?' I said, 'Why ask me? I don't know any Americans.' She said, 'You know this one.' Then she said—get this, 'During the War there was a type called Alexis Bodine around Provence. You worked with him. Tell me about him.' So she knows McCarey is Bodine!"

"A lot of people know that now. What did you tell her?"

"I told her what a rat this Bodine is. But you ought to see her. If she likes you, she'll tell you about Pateck and Barodi. You want her phone number?"

I called the number Bernard gave me, which was in Cannes, and Suzie answered immediately. Her voice on the phone was low and husky, loaded with sex. I told her I was the one she had seen at St. Tropez at the little café on the *quai* and that I wanted to see her.

"Where did you get my telephone number?" she asked.

I told her. "Bernard is an old friend. I knew him during the War."

"Well, all right. Where are you?"

"St. Raphael. No. 8 rue Honoré-Vadon, Apartment 15, on the top floor."

"Wait a minute. Let me write it down. . . . Fine. But I haven't a car. I wrecked mine."

"Take a taxi. I'll pay for it."

"You must be loaded. O.K., I'll see you in about an hour."

I went back to my peeping-tom business on the Hotel Nouvel, using a pair of 7 x 42 Habicht binoculars which I had found in a cupboard when I had searched the apartment. I saw two males in the room Pete had occupied the last day of his life. One was a portly gent of middle age who was egg-bald and might have been a Turk. He went about the room in long underwear that needed laundering and he had a nervous habit of scratching his privates. Or maybe it wasn't a nervous habit. His companion was a plump boy of sixteen or seventeen with a loose, wet mouth that hung open most of the time. I would have given ten to one he was the old party's punk. He looked the part. His walk was feminine and he kept his eyes languidly half-closed in a way that's supposed to be sexy. For all I know, it is.

The room under this was occupied by a couple who were dressing to go out. The wife, if she was a wife, looked to be in her twenties but already had too large a stomach that was almost grotesque with her spindly legs. But her face was pretty and doll-like with small, regular features and big eyes with plenty of mascara. It was the man who interested me. He was swarthy and mean-looking and he wore a shoulder holster under his shirt with what looked like the butt of a German Luger sticking out. He was another one such as Pateck, but without Pateck's polish. I spent a long time studying his features and I had a strong feeling that I had seen him somewhere before. I was certain it wasn't recently. I damned my memory, which once had been so infallible. I dug as deeply as I knew how but I could come up with nothing.

They were dressed and their light went out. The Turk had closed his shutters. The rest of the windows were shuttered. Or dark. I put the binoculars away and stretched out on the divan. Three cigarettes later there was a knocking on the door. I jumped up and opened it. There stood Suzie Lautrey in a black silk sheath that caressed every curve of her, a mink held negligently in her left hand and resting on the floor, an unlit cigarette in her carmine mouth, and a small, pearl-handled automatic in her right hand which she pointed right at my eyes. I guess I left my mouth open. She pulled the trigger and a flame jumped up from the top of the little gun. It was a cigarette lighter. I closed my mouth. I took the gadget from her and lit her cigarette. I handed it back to her and said, "Won't you come in?"

She swept past me, grinning, got to the center of the living room, dropped her coat on the floor, then turned to regard me. She said, "I know the kind of men I like. One look is all I need. Come here and kiss me."

I did what the lady asked. I'll tell you something: It's very seldom that American men get kissed like that.

"Where's the bedroom?" she asked.

I said, "Look, sweetheart, keep your clothes on a few minutes. I've got something important to talk to you about."

"Can't we talk—after?"

"Let's talk now. You want a drink?"

"Certainly not. Do you think I want to spoil things?"

"Just asking. . . . Won't you sit down?"

"No. I'm not going to talk that long. Go ahead. What is it?"

"What were you doing out with that ape Pateck?"

"Ape is right!" She laughed. "I can't stand men like that!"

"What were you doing with him then?"

"I was doing a favor for a friend."

"A favor, eh?"

She pointed to the mink on the floor. "I got that," she said. "Do you think you could match it?"

"I don't have to match it," I said. "I'm not going to ask you for any favors."

She laughed again. She snatched the small silk hat from her head and threw it on the divan, then ran her fingers through her auburn hair. "I'm the one that's going to ask for the favor."

"Oh?"

She said in a low, caressing voice, "Make love to me

sweetly, darling. Please make love to me sweetly and gently. Please. . . ."

She did have a sexy voice. She packed enough sex into that 'please' to blow the top of my head off. Brother, had I gotten in deep!

"All right," I said, "but first, a word from our sponsor. I want you to tell me about Sandor Barodi."

The smile left her lips, the hot eyes suddenly cooled to icy green. Gone was all of the love play, the mischievousness. Her body which she had held beautifully straight sagged in the middle. She walked slowly to the divan and sat down, looking at me as though I had hurt her. She said, "Do you always do that—stick pins into little girls' balloons?"

"I didn't intend it that way," I said apologetically. "I think I used to know this Barodi, before he was a count and before he had his great wealth. . . . I know you are a friend of his. I just wanted to hear you talk about him."

She ran her hand over her forehead, then looked at it. She kicked off her Italian slippers and curled her feet under her. She said, "Barodi owns me. I hate him, I detest him, I vomit when I say his name, but he owns me, just as he owns his little French poodle Lippi. What else do you want to know? . . ."

"I guess that's enough, Suzie. . . . I'm sorry. You were so happy when you came in here."

"Sit down beside me," she said. "I'll tell you about Sandor Barodi. Why shouldn't I? . . . You're Alexis Bodine, aren't you? He told me about you. He told me that Pateck would point you out to me and that I was to meet you and make love to you and report everything that happened and everything you said. Barodi told me you were a killer. He told me you were the most vicious son of a bitch alive. Also he told me that it was you who massacred the three men at the Villa Le Trayas."

I nodded at her. "There is some truth in what he has told you, Suzie."

She shook her head violently. "I know better!" she exclaimed. "Do you think that I did not mean what I said when I came in here? I do know the kind of men I like. Also, I know good men from evil men. Barodi is an evil

111

man. Aldo de Lys is evil—Pateck is evil. These are the evil ones! You are not. You are a silly romantic. And even if you do violent things, you do them because you believe you are right. . . . Men in wartime do violent things and they are not evil. That is the way you are."

"You have found all of that in my face?" I asked.

"No, just confirmation. Aristide Bernard told me about you—what you had done for France during the War and how you had used your own money to feed the poor and find homes for the orphaned children afterwards. . . . I know a lot about you, Alexis Bodine."

"Well—now what do we do? You are owned by Barodi."

She jumped up from the divan and pointed a finger at my nose. "I'll tell you what we'll do," she said. She started to undress with furious speed. She unzipped the sheath and took it off over her head. Underneath was a black silk petticoat and she got out of that. She stood in black panties and black bra. She rolled down her stockings and tossed them aside. She unhooked the bra and tossed it on the divan, revealing beautifully firm breasts of a delectable size. Then she stepped out of her panties, wadded them up, and threw them at me. "Does any of this give you an idea about what we're going to do?" she asked.

She was a beautiful animal—and at that moment I believed she was the most stunningly beautiful I have ever seen. But I didn't have any desire for her and the Lord knows I didn't need her, with the feel of Tita so recent in my arms.

"Put 'em back on," I said. "You don't have to prove anything to me."

"Prove anything?"

"Yes, that you're the sexiest charge since Aphrodite. I'm just not interested."

She looked at me out of those green eyes and I set myself for some sort of violence. Hysterics was the least I expected. You just don't reject girls like Suzie. . . . She suddenly smiled and nodded her head in a knowing way. "Martita de Castro?" she asked.

"Yes," I said, "It's Martita and no one else."

She came over to me and she put her hand on me. Then she backed away and studied me for a moment. "You

112

know, I think you really mean that. . . . Well, I'll be damned!"

She retrieved her panties from the floor at my feet and she put them on. Then she picked up her bra.

"Thanks, angel," I said.

She had her head bent hooking her bra. When she straightened up I saw there were tears in her eyes.

15

IF ANYTHING WAS DEVELOPING, I didn't know about it. Outside of importing Pateck and sicking Suzie on me, they were making none of the moves I would have expected. And not only that, I still didn't know who "they" were, beyond Barodi. It would have seemed to me, the way we had conducted this business a few years ago, that preparations would have been made for my extermination, just as they had exterminated Pete Dumbrowsky. As the days passed, I began to wonder if my sortie into the Villa Le Trayas had not been a wasted gesture. . . . It was certainly wasted if it had invited no more trouble than Pateck and Suzie.

I heard from Tita every night by phone and she would recount in detail her day's excursion to the couturiers and the shops and any adventures that befell. She was having a good time spending the money I had given her. Also she didn't want to come back to the Riviera. She didn't say so, but I knew her well enough at least to deduce that attitude from her gay telephone chatting. I think that she was afraid of the Côte d'Azur, not only because of Vico del Oro but even more so because of my own activities. Now that she was safely away, she wanted no more of them. . . . And I think she was afraid of me, too. I think that she had begun to have doubts about me after the massacre at Le Trayas. There was nothing I could put my finger on; it was merely that she seemed to have changed in some subtle ways—in ways so subtle that I could not even describe

113

them. It was just a feeling, no more than that. You are very sensitive to a woman you have been as close to as I had been to Tita.

The daily reports from Fox Group were particularly unrevealing. The Baron de Lys had been traced to Baden-Baden where he was taking daily baths. Nothing of interest was happening at the Hotel Nouvel. Pateck was in Room 207. He was seen frequently in a Vedette parked on the rue Honoré-Vadon near the hotel. The license number was G-28099. He was probably waiting for me to come out of No. 8. But he didn't follow me on my morning sorties for *croissants* and milk. Only at night when I went out to dinner, which I did seldom. Sergeant Luchon reported that the search for the Le Trayas assassin finally had been called off and that they were once more having coffee in the guardroom. Also that Delacroix of the *Sûreté* had been absent from the Riviera for over a week and was believed to be in Paris conferring with his superiors. Bernard told me that Vico del Oro had gone back to Corsica after two days at Antibes. Also he said that the portly gent in the top floor room at the Nouvel with the boy was not a Turk but Abdul-el-Krim, a coffee and spice merchant from Oran. It was Bernard's opinion that this was a Krim from Damascus. My hours at the window with the binoculars had disclosed one new fact about this Krim—that at five-thirty or thereabouts every evening he gave himself a hypodermic injection high on the right buttock. Also I discovered that the doll-faced blonde on the floor below ate chocolates constantly, which might have accounted for her big belly.

Then I got an unsigned and perfumed note in the mail, which the concierge brought up to me Monday evening. It read, "S. B. is furious!!! When are you going to make love to me?"

That was a good question, what with Tita staying in Paris so long. However, I could certainly hold out against Suzie if I didn't see her. . . . I called the number at Cannes and a man answered. He was abrupt and unfriendly. He said, "Who do you want?"

"I'd like to speak to Mlle. Lautrey," I said.

"Who is this calling?"

"The Baron de Lys."

"Aldo? . . . You are not Aldo! Who are you?"

Then I heard Suzie's voice say indignantly, "Stop that!" and a hand was put over the phone. I listened for two minutes. Nothing. Then suddenly there was a loud bang in my ear and I heard voices dimly in angry argument. There was a slam, as of a door, and Suzie said, "Hello?"

"This is Alex Bodine."

"Alex! I hoped you'd call! I had a feeling it was you the way that pig was talking!"

"What pig, angel?"

"That Vico! I can't stand him, snooping around like a dog in heat!"

"Vico del Oro, eh? I thought he was in Corsica."

"He flew over for the big ball Wednesday night. He wanted me to go with him. Ugh! I'd rather go with a snake. Besides, I think now that you are going to take me."

"Take you to a ball? Not me, honey."

"Alex, you've got to! Its the *bal du printemps* at El Dorado—the only affair of any importance this season. It's a *bal masqué et costumé* and no one will know you, if that's what's worrying you. We can—"

"At El Dorado, you say?" I interrupted.

"Yes, the Count Barodi gives it every year for the children's hospital at St. Laurent. We can dress up like crazy and we can have a lot of fun. I'll make you a costume. I'm a very talented designer, if it's something useless like that."

"Well, I might at that. We won't say anything to Barodi. We can surprise him."

"What a surprise!" she said. "He'll flip!"

She wanted to come over to St. Raphael right away. I vetoed that.

"But I have to take your measurements!" she said. "How can I make you a costume if I don't know how big you are?"

"Just guess, honey. Make it roomy enough, that's all."

"No! We do this my way or we don't do it. I'm coming over. Besides I've got a new white Jaguar and I've got to give it a ride. You wait there."

She hung up before I could protest further. And to be truthful, I don't really know whether I wanted to protest further. I cared nothing about her emotionally, to be sure,

115

but she was a human being and I was getting starved for human companionship. She liked me, and it's difficult to keep pushing away those who like you. Also and incidentally, she was the most gorgeous scenery on the Riviera and I was in a mood to look at scenery. The fact that she was finally going to lead me to Barodi under uniquely favorable circumstances was what you might call a happy coincidence.

She was knocking at my door within half an hour. That was a fast Jag she had bought—or had given to her. She had a green scarf around her head upon which were printed in gold various mottos and sayings of a suggestive nature; she wore a green suede jacket and bottle-green shorts. She was barefooted. She came into my living room and she took off her jacket. She had on a white cashmere sweater that didn't harm the scenery a bit. She took a tape measure from her jacket pocket and she said, "All right, now, let's get down to business."

I said, "Aren't you going to make any lewd suggestions?"

She shook her head. "No, I was over that road the other night. I made up my mind coming over here. I decided that either you make the passes at me or to hell with you. I don't need you."

"How about Barodi?"

"I don't need him either. I can make out anywhere in this world."

"Yes, you can at that, Suzie."

"So stop talking about it. Put up or shut up. Now come here, you monkey, and let me see how big you are."

She measured me expertly, jotting down notations in a small leather-bound notebook with a gold pencil.

"What are we going to be?" I asked.

"I haven't decided yet. I wanted to see what you thought. There's no limit, really. We could go as a couple of the seasons—Spring and Fall, or Winter and Summer—we could be lovers out of poetry or history—we could represent great paintings or comic characters or Greek mythology or songs or—anything. What would you like?"

"I'll leave it up to you. Why don't you surprise me?"

"Just like a man! You're too lazy to think of anything so you pass the buck to me!"

116

"Only one thing, darling, I'll have to have my back covered and my upper legs. I've got scars that would be too easy to identify, in some quarters."

"Scars? What from?"

"A beating."

"Recently?"

"Three weeks or so ago. Also, I think that it would be best if our costumes weren't too sensational—we should blend in with the others. What costumes does one usually see at these balls?"

"Look. Who beat you?"

"A couple of hoodlums. You'd look good in a tutu. That's what I'd like to see you in. With those legs of yours, you'll stop all of the traffic."

"I guess that's the story of the Villa Le Trayas, eh?" she asked.

I shrugged at her. "That's yesterday's pot of beans. Let's talk about the costumes."

She sat on the divan and I lit a cigarette for her. She curled her legs under her and she patted the cushion beside her for me to join her. "I like the idea of the tutu," she said. "A girl can run fast in a tutu, and with some of these goats at Barodi's parties, you either run fast or else."

"Fine. I saw a ballet some years ago about a street girl and an apache—'The Girl Who Ate Diamonds' or some such. You be the street girl and I'll be the apache."

"That's too corny. Half the Riviera delinquents will come as street girls and apaches. I'll be the Sleeping Beauty—who woke up—and you be the Prince. I'll do you up stinking, with satin tights and a big white blouse with sequins all over it and an ermine cape. . . . That way, you'll have room to pack a gun under your arm."

I said, "Who's side are you on, angel?"

"I'm on your side—when I'm with you. I'd like to be on your side all the time, but you don't want me."

I let it lay there. What could I tell her that would be honest that she'd want to hear?

That night I told Tita on the phone that I was going to the *bal au printemps*.

"Of all things!" she exclaimed. "Why?"

117

"I have business with Barodi, and this seems to be a convenient way to conduct it."

"You have business with Uncle Sandor? Not about me!"

"No, other business."

"You don't want to tell me?"

"No."

"Who are you going with?"

"Suzie. That redhead I told you about."

"With Suzie!" There was a long silence. Then she asked, "You have been seeing her?"

"Not in any way that needs explaining. Strictly business."

"I don't like your business," she said. "I don't like it at all, Alex. I'm going to say good-bye now. I've got a lot of things to think about."

"Listen, darling, please don't—"

"Good-bye," she said, and the phone clicked, then hummed a derisive note in my ear.

I thought a long time about calling her back. I didn't.

On Tuesday I phoned Bernard at Grasse and told him a part of my plan. I said that I wanted to use Dohaine's boat Wednesday and Wednesday night, and that he was to arrange to have gas enough with him to cruise about a hundred and fifty miles. Also some machine guns, such as Sten guns or larger. "Get at least two of them and plenty of ammunition."

"O.K.," he said. "Do you want a crew?"

"No, just Dohaine."

"I can take tomorrow off," he pleaded. "I'd like to go along as crew."

"It won't be anything," I said. "Just sitting around and waiting."

"I'll be along, then. What time will you be leaving St. Tropez?"

"About noon. See you."

Tita didn't phone me Tuesday night. I tried to get her but her hotel room didn't answer.

Suzie called me Wednesday noon to report that my costume would be ready in a couple of hours. "I've got two women sewing it," she said. "I think you're going to like it."

"Fine. I'll be over about four and try it on."

"No, I'll bring it to you at St. Raphael."

"I'd rather go to your apartment, Suzie."

"No men come to my apartment."

"No? How about Vico, angel?"

"He wasn't invited! He forced his way in! That pig!"

"Won't you make an exception for me?"

There was a long silence. Finally she said, "It's on the avenue de la Liberté, facing the port. Number 14, third floor, Apartment 32. I'll tell the concierge, otherwise she won't let you up. That pig of a Vico!"

"O.K. About four o'clock, then."

"And you be nice to me, you son of a bitch!"

I left No. 8 at eleven o'clock, Wednesday. I drove in a leisurely fashion to Frejus and caught several glimpses of Pateck's Vedette following me. I took the road to Ste. Maxime and stepped on the Citroën's tail. It was a good road car and I wound it up to a hundred on the straight stretches. The Vedette kept up fairly well, but I sensed that Pateck was in difficulties when he encountered traffic. He didn't take the close chances while passing slower cars. He was too cautious. He wanted to live too long. So I left him out of sight west of Ste. Maxime and I turned into the St. Tropez road unobserved.

I didn't kid myself about that. He would come to St. Tropez all right. That would be the first place he'd hunt for me. But I wasn't going to make it easy for him.

Also, I didn't kid myself about the boat. I'd ditched them once by sea and I was certain they wouldn't let me get away with it a second time. They'd surely have a boat standing by to watch *le Bouc*. That isn't why I wanted the boat. When you start shooting on the water, you don't have a lot of witnesses around and you don't have the police interfering. I had to set up a gallery, just in case there was going to be shooting.

I parked the Citroën in a garage near the *quai*, then walked to Dohaine's boat. He was sitting on the stone wall smoking a cigarette. He got up and we shook hands.

119

"Bernard around?" I asked.

"He's down in the cabin. I think he's seasick already."

"Let's take off. Maybe we can get away before Pateck shows up. I left him back on the road. Keep an eye open for him. He's driving a gray Vedette."

We went aboard and Dohaine started the engine. I cast off the lines, then went to the cabin. Bernard was stretched out on the settee. He got up, stretched and yawned, then shook hands solemnly.

"You feeling all right?" I asked him.

"Fine. Just tired. I had one of those nights."

"Oh?"

"Yes. There's a new girl at the Coq d'Or and we got to talking about politics—she's a *Poujardiste*, if you can imagine that!—and drinking brandy, and before I knew it we were in a hotel room. . . . Well! If it's just waiting we're going to do, I'll have plenty of time to sleep."

"When are you going to stop chasing women, Bernard?"

"Me? I hope never!"

We went up to the bridge together. Dohaine reported there was no sign of a Vedette or of Pateck. He pointed to another boat tied up around the *quai* from his own berth. "They've started their engine," he said. "That's *la Mouette*. She'll be casting off in a moment and following us. They've been dogging me every time I've gone out since that trip we took to Ste. Maxime."

"Who's boat is it?" I asked.

"Belongs to old Cassgraine. He's chartered it to some city folks. Have their own captain."

"How many of them?"

"Usually three or four. They've got four aboard now."

"Can you outrun her?"

"We're a little faster, but not enough to ditch her in a short run."

"How about from here to Cannes?"

"We could leave her all right."

"Then let's do it. Let's go to Cannes. I've got a date there at four."

16

WE SWUNG INTO THE HARBOR at Cannes at three-thirty
and tied up at the *quai* alongside the Municipal Casino
after Bernard had shown his police badge and I had given a
one-thousand-franc tip to the watchman. We were behind
a 100-ton diesel yacht called the *Olympus* in Greek letters
and flying a Greek flag at her stern, in violation of the custom for moored yachts. We were well hidden from the sea
and from most of the rest of the harbor, so if *la Mouette*
wanted to find us they'd have to come all the way in.

"You wait," I told Dohaine and Bernard. "I'm going to
one of those buildings over there—No. 14, third floor,
Apartment 32, in the name of Lautrey. Vico del Oro is on
the loose around here somewhere, so if you don't hear from
me I'll be full of his buckshot. Otherwise I'll see you around
eight and we'll take a boat ride."

Bernard said, "Weren't you the one making cracks about
me chasing women?"

I didn't deign to answer. I didn't have an answer. Not a
ready one. I walked across the *quai*, found No. 14, and told
the concierge my name. She shooed me to an open-work
elevator and I rode to the third *étage*. Suzie opened the
door to my knock. She had on what you might call lounging
pajamas, of silk so sheer that you could tell she wasn't a
real redhead. But I knew that.

She said, "Well, stop gaping and come in."

I walked into the den of the Sybarite—that's precisely
the way it was decorated. It was made for luxurious lounging, for the utmost in the comfort of a hedonist, and it was
as feminine as a two-way stretch girdle. The color scheme
was pastel—what you might call sensationally soothing. The
furniture was good Danish modern with an oriental profusion of pillows to hide the square corners. It was a room
that went with Suzie Lautrey like the whiff of Joy that followed her every passage. She sat down on a white carpet of

ankle-deep pile and picked up a fluffy bundle of light green lace upon which she was sewing. Her fingers flew as she plied the needle. She said, "Take off your shoes and make yourself at home. I'll be just a few minutes with this."

I walked around the room and looked at her pictures. There were a couple of Picassos, a Montmartre Utrillo, a Paul Ullman, and a mess of neo-this's-and-that's. The door was open so I wandered into the bedroom. Black and silver. If anyone had described it to me, I wouldn't have believed it. And yet it was a delightful room. But it was difficult to keep your attention concentrated on the room once you were inside. Covering almost an entire wall was a nude of Suzie—the sexiest nude I have ever seen of any woman by an artist. She was standing in a green cape which was tied around her neck with a cord and thrown back over her shoulders. In her right hand was a fencing foil, the tip resting on the floor. On her glowing face was the look of a woman in the act of love, and her entire beautiful body followed the mood of that look. Brother!

I sat on the black lace-covered bed and gaped at it. A voice said in my ear, "Do you like it?"

I turned around and there was Suzie bending over the bed. The sheer silk showed the pink of her nipples. I got up and walked into the living room. She followed me, grinning.

"Well?" she asked.

"It's so beautiful it's obscene," I said. "Christ! Who did that?"

"A little Pan sort of fairy by the name of Zeno. He's never made love to a woman in his life, but he has theories about it."

"He sure as hell has," I agreed.

"Your costume's in that box," she said, pointing to a cardboard container resting amid the pillows on the sofa. "You try it on. I'm going to take a bath. If you want to wash me, you come in. It's that door."

She left me abruptly. She meant what she had said back at St. Raphael. Either I made the passes or the hell with me. She didn't need me. I sat on the sofa next to the box and tried to think things out. I did want her, despite everything I had told myself and her. I wanted her more every

122

time I saw her. But it wasn't a mere arithmetical progression—it was geometric. It was the square of the desire multiplied by the seeing, and then the whole kit and kaboodle raised to the nth power. It was getting right to the point of torture to look at her and be near her and to keep my hands off her. But it wasn't torture yet. I could still hold out. I was still safe if I didn't see her another time. I was going to be all right for tonight, I told myself. I lit a cigarette, kicked off my shoes and put my feet up on the coffee table. I didn't want to think of Tita. Somehow it would seem to be a sacrilege to bring the thought of her into this den. I compared her apartment in St. Raphael with this and I knew which I preferred. You couldn't spend your days in this profusion of sensation. A home was just a background to its people. Of course it had to be comfortable, but only to a degree. The real comfort was in your companionship—in the mutual warmth that emanated from two people in love. You didn't need to decorate that comfort with laces and satins and cushions and rugs and Danish modern. . . . I lit another cigarette. I talked to myself some more about Suzie's apartment and the kind of a girl it would predicate. I decided that I didn't like this Suzie at all, when you came right down to it. Of course I was drawn to her, but that was mere animalism. Sex. Fornication. She was the kind of girl you fornicated with, which had nothing to do with making love, despite the acceptably inaccurate interchange of terms. There was no substance to her when she wasn't seducing you or loving you—no, there was that "love" again—fornicating with you. And sometimes you needed that too, but not when you had a dear love like Tita. . . . Well, it was settled then. I wouldn't wash her.

I put out my cigarette, stripped to my shorts and put on the costume. The pants were dark purple satin with gold lace stripe down the sides and fitted perfectly, skin-tight around the thighs and waist. The patent-leather boots were my size. The white satin shirt was roomy but too swishy, with lace on the collar and cuffs. The sequined white mohair jacket was just too much. The ermine cape I didn't put on. Suzie came out of her bathroom in a black lace negligee with nothing on underneath and oo'd and ah'd over me. She made me put on the ermine and a white

123

shako which she got out of another box on the floor. Then she adjusted my black mask and led me to her bedroom to have a look at myself. Right out of Victor Herbert! But I was impressed nevertheless. I even got to feel comfortable in the ermine cape.

"You're beautiful!" Suzie exclaimed. "All of the girls are going to wet themselves when they see you!" She felt around my ribs and shook her head. "Where's your gun?"

"In my suit pocket."

"Aren't you going to take it?"

"Sure. I'll find some place for it."

"It should be in a shoulder holster. I had the blouse and shirt made big enough. . . . Haven't you got one?"

I shook my head. She went to a chest of drawers and opened the top one. She took out a contraption of straps and a ball of mink fur. "Try this," she said.

I looked at it unbelieving. A mink gun holster! "Whose was this?"

"Never mind. I got it for you."

"You're very thoughtful, Suzie. Whom do you want me to shoot?"

"Barodi, if you've got the guts."

"It isn't a question of guts. I'd have to have a reason and the opportunity."

"I'll give you a reason! . . ." She sat on the bed and put her head in her hands. Then she looked up and frowned at me. "No, don't listen to me. I'm crazy today. I'm afraid of myself when I get like this. . . . You're bad for me, Alex Bodine! You give me a false sense of importance. You make me feel like—like a person!" Suddenly she broke into a fit of sobbing, burying her head in her arms on the bed. I sat beside her and rubbed the nape of her neck with my fingers.

"I'm not a person—I'm nothing!" she said between sobs. "Just something to be used by filthy, horrible pigs of men! I'm so disgusted with myself! I've made such a mess of my life!"

I mumbled some inanities at her. I told her how beautiful she was—how she had her whole life before her. Things like that. She shook her head violently. "You don't know what you're talking about! Pollyanna! My life! I've killed

124

everything I've ever loved! I've killed everyone who has ever loved me! I'm death, I tell you! Death!"

She was on the verge of hysteria. What for? What had suddenly taken hold of her like this? I stood up and looked at her writhing in agony, fighting through some obscure personal hell. She sat up suddenly and looked at me as though I were a hated opponent. "What are you doing in my bedroom?" she screamed. "Get out! Get out!"

I went out and closed the bedroom door. I took off the mask, the shako, the cape and the blouse. I sat down on the divan and lit a cigarette. I thought about Suzie. And I thought about a girl I had known in 1946 in Teheran who went by the single name of Sonia and danced in a vulgar and exciting way in a small *boîte* called la Nuit d'Amour. Sonia had often done exactly what Suzie was doing—she had blown her top at me. I had to be with her on many of these occasions because she was the Bu-X contact with a certain Russian gentleman we were interested in. Sonia had a simple cure for her break-ups—a needleful of heroin.

I sat and I smoked my cigarette and I waited. There was no sound from the bedroom. Then the door opened quietly and Suzie came into the living room, still in her black lace negligee. She smiled at me in a most friendly way and she said, "What are you doing out here, you ape? Why don't you come into the bedroom and help me try on my costume?"

Her eyes were a little brighter than usual—that's all.

We took *le Bouc* to Antibes. There had been an argument about that. Suzie didn't want to go for a boat ride, she said. And then when we got to Antibes, how would we get to El Dorado, which was high on the mountain overlooking the sea? And what was wrong with her new white Jaguar? And why wouldn't I do just one teeny little thing that she wanted? Not one thing had I done that she had asked me since she had known me—not one!

We rode down in the open-work elevator at eight-thirty, Suzie talking and me listening. She wasn't really upset about anything—she was just in the mood to make a fuss. . . . Maybe the effect of the needle was wearing off too quickly. Maybe she hadn't given herself a big enough charge.

She had on her tutu—a really beautiful creation in pale green—a skirt as fluffy as meringue and a bodice encrusted with rhinestones. She wore a diamond collar that looked like a mobster's ransom, and a bracelet to match. But there was no red hair. She had on a black wig so expertly made and fitted that even close scrutiny could not detect it. On top of her new hair was a small rhinestone crown, well made. She was sensational as a brunette. The dark hair gave a new contrast to her green eyes and seemed to change her entire personality. She had on net stockings which did everything for her legs a lily-gilder could dream up, and on her feet were silver evening slippers. She had scoffed at my suggestion of ballet flats. "Flats are as square as your head," she had said. She had her mink coat over her bare shoulders and she carried a white cashmere scarf and her pale green mask in her hand.

I was back in my St. Tropez suit, carrying my costume in its boxes. This had caused another argument when I had announced I was going to change on the boat. She had summed up her feelings about that with a French phrase that doesn't translate very well. What it amounts to is that I was a kind of a residue of something unsavory. Let's let it go at that.

She was surprised to see Bernard on the boat and she greeted him effusively. She took a fast tour of the cabin, the galley and the bridge with him, then came to the after-deck and announced that she was pleased with *le Bouc* and she was very glad we had decided to go to Antibes by sea. "After all, how many of these Riviera slobs will arrive on their yachts?" she asked.

We got underway immediately. I went up to the bridge with Dohaine and I asked him if *la Mouette* had shown up. He pointed to the other side of the harbor. "She's over there, beside that schooner. She was towed in about an hour ago by the lifeguards. Bernard strolled over there and found out they had had engine trouble. But it was nothing serious. They'll be along, all right, and we won't outrun them by far to Antibes. It's too close."

I went down to the cabin. Suzie had settled on the settee amid the pillows and cushions and Bernard was drooling

126

around her making her comfortable. I gave him the office to scram. I got a bottle of champagne out of the cooler in the galley and filled two glasses. I sat down by Suzie's feet and I said, "This is a good quiet place to talk. I'd like to ask you something, Suzie."

She sipped her champagne and batted her eyelashes at me. She put her legs on my knee and said, "Go ahead, darling."

I said, "You got a mink coat for Pateck. What did you get the Jaguar for?"

She laughed and spilled some wine on her arm. She put a finger in it, then leaned over and rubbed the finger behind my ear. "*Merde,*" she said, "That's for luck."

"I'll need it. Now how about the Jaguar, angel?"

"I got that for you—for bringing you to the ball!"

"But you already have the Jaguar and I'm not at the ball yet."

"It's a cinch. . . . I knew I'd get you there, and so did Barodi. You know, darling, you're tough all right, and I must say you haven't made love to me—yet. But otherwise and when it comes to women, you're as soft as a custard pudding. . . . I just thought you'd like to know that."

"Fine. You keep on believing that, angel—you and Barodi. Now one other thing, did you tell Barodi about our costumes—what we'd be wearing?"

She shook her head. "No. That wasn't a part of the agreement. But he'll find out quick enough."

"Yes, I suppose he will. What time do we all unmask? Not at midnight?"

"Much later than that. Not until two o'clock. That's the custom at Barodi's parties. The party goes all night—and sometimes all day and all the next night. It depends."

"On what?"

"On what sort of mood he's in. If he's in the mood for a party, then we have a party."

"And the mink gun holster, angel, did he give you that?"

"No, he doesn't know about that either. I took that away from Vico when he crashed into my apartment. I took his gun, too."

"So he's carrying a gun now! . . . But I wanted to talk to

you about something much more important than any of this. I've been thinking a lot about it and I believe I've got it worked out. Angel, you were in St. Raphael on April 18 last about three-thirty or four o'clock in the afternoon, weren't you?"

"I was—what? How would I know where I was on any certain day? April the eighteenth! Phooey!"

"Let me put it another way, then. On this April 18 you had a rendezvous at the hotel in St. Raphael with a certain man—an American. Would you remember that?"

She sipped her wine and didn't look at me. I lit a couple of cigarettes and handed her one. Her eyes met mine as she took it from my hand. There seemed to be a stricken look in them. . . . Maybe it was just my imagination. How would I know what a stricken look looks like?

"You knew Pete Dumbrowsky, didn't you?" I asked her.

She kept her head down and I couldn't see into her face. She said, "I don't want to talk about him."

"He was a friend of mine, angel. Why don't you want to talk about him?"

"Because. . . . Because I loved him. Because he was the one man I loved."

"You loved him? Are you sure?"

"Yes, I'm sure."

She looked up at me then and her eyes were wet with tears. My God, maybe she had loved him!

"Will you tell me one other thing, angel?"

"What?"

"At this hotel—this Hotel Nouvel—who else was with you besides Pete?"

"Nobody else. No, nobody."

"You are lying to me, angel. Do you want me to tell you the name of this other man?"

She put out her hand in a gesture of appeal. Now the look on her face *was* stricken. You couldn't mistake it. She choked back a sob, then said in a whisper, "Please—please don't torture me with that! I can't stand it! I'll—I'll have to kill myself! My God, don't you understand that I can hardly live with myself now! I can't stand it. I tell you, I can't stand it!"

She bent over into the cushions and started to sob. I

stood up and looked at her, wondering how violent this break-up was going to become.

I hoped she had brought her needle along. . . .

17

WE WERE IN Antibes Harbor within an hour. I was a white Prince Charming and Mlle. Suzanne Lautrey was a pale green Sleeping Beauty, and we got into an ancient Delahaye cab Bernard had rustled up in the town and we rode with practically no pomp up the mountainside to the villa of the Count Sandor Barodi. Suzie was gay again—and quite bright-eyed—and she seemed to have no memory of the discussion of Pete Dumbrowsky and its accompanying emotional storm. She was just a beautiful girl being very affectionate toward her male companion and there was nothing on her mind but a night of play. . . . That's the way she seemed.

We arrived early, which was the way Suzie wanted it, and there were no more than fifty motor equipages in front of the white marble palace in which Barodi nested.

This Villa El Dorado was in the traditional style of French royal residences and was not actually as imposing from the exterior as the Villa Le Trayas. It was more than double the size of de Lys' villa, built around a *cour carré*, but the face it presented to the world was sober and even modest, if such adjectives can be applied to palaces. Everything of any account was inside, where it belonged.

What there was inside was a ballroom which made that at Versailles seem shabby. This room was more than two stories high, with a vaulted ceiling, gold leafed and sculptured. Hanging low were three huge crystal chandeliers of such brilliance and beauty that you were dazzled. The ballroom was Louis XIV at its best—gold and crystal and mirrors, with a parquet floor of intricate geometrical design that looked like the top of an oriental table. At each end of the room were orchestras on raised platforms, and against the far wall was a gleaming white buffet table sixty feet long and loaded with all of the foods, the wines, the liquers and other spirits that could have been imagined by a desert island castaway—that is, a castaway who had been at the very least a Prince of Araby.

A butler announced, "Prince Charming and the Sleeping Beauty," as we entered the ballroom, and then we were greeted by a huge bear of a man dressed as a Barbary pirate, with a bandolier of shells across his barrel of a chest and two pistols stuck into his black sash that seemed to be more modern than the costume called for. Beside him was a Saracen slavegirl in golden chains and a tunic cut low enough to reveal her ample and beautiful breasts. The pirate kissed Suzie's hand, bowing low, then shook mine and bade us welcome. The slave girl also shook our hands and she stuck the tip of her tongue out at me and said, "You're a big one!"

As we walked away, Suzie's arm in mine, I distinctly heard the pirate say, "Those are more beautiful legs than Suzie's. I wonder who that one is?"

I asked Suzie, "Who are they?"

"That's Ludwig Starbruck. He's the Count's closest companion—sort of major domo. He runs everything. That girl is Candée Deprez—you've seen her in the movies, I'm sure. She always plays the part of a whore. Type casting."

"No friend of yours, eh?"

"I saw her stick out her tongue at you! . . . I told you what would happen when the girls saw you in this costume!"

We danced a slow fox-trot over to the buffet table. I was beginning to remember that I hadn't had any dinner. Suzie took a plate with caviar and biscuits and champagne. I got some *pâté de foi*, black bread, and a glass of Barsac. We found a couple of chairs in an alcove. I said, "What's the plot?"

"I've no idea. You're here. I'm here. And I've got my Jaguar."

"We play it by ear, then. When does the Great Man make his entrance?"

"Probably much later than this. I hear there's a big meeting going on, and besides he's got a new girl, an Indian actress by the name of Melanie Rudra, or some such, and they make love after dinner. That's an old Indian custom. She's very dark and as curvy as the road to Menton. She wears diamonds on each nostril—right here—and she's got little feet and thick ankles. . . . I think he got the idea from reading about Rosselini. Those Italians!"

We finished our *hors-d'oeuvres,* then went back for something substantial. Suzie took roast pheasant and more champagne; I tried Westphalian ham, hot potato salad, and Nuits St. George. We returned to our alcove and watched the dancers and ate. The revelers were arriving in a steady stream now and the ballroom was filling up. It was a wonderfully colorful throng and there was great imagination shown in many of the costumes. Also there were any number of nudes, very near, semi and demi, both male and female, and some of these wore obscene arrangements of body-parts to depict the nightmares that surrealists enjoy. The general atmosphere very soon became bacchanalian and the cries of nymphs in ecstacy and/or distress were not infrequently heard above the orchestra.

Suzie said, "Let's dance. I need some exercise after all that food." We waltzed half way around the ballroom and a big green frog tapped me on the shoulder and said, "May I?" Suzie said, "Yes, he may—if you don't mind," and I relinquished her. . . . I guess she was finding it pretty dull with me, and I'll admit I wasn't in a mood that you'd call playful.

I was waiting for something to happen and I was quite certain that it was going to happen to me and that, unless I could conjure up a genuine inspiration, I would have no control over it at all. I hunted around for inspiration; I noted each door and each alcove and I took a closer look at the various males wandering about alone. . . . There were an unusual number of Barbary pirates with bandoliers and pistols in their waistbands and several of them just stood and watched and seemed to take no part in the revelry. I spotted Suzie coming around in my direction and I started toward her to cut in when suddenly I saw something that stopped me dead. This was another ballerina, in a white Swan Lake costume with a feathered hat on her head and a jeweled mask, and she was dancing very close

131

to a cat-like youth attired as a toreador. There was a clear space on the floor for an instant and I saw her slim, supple body and long, graceful legs that made Suzie's curved and dimpled ones look vulgar. Then the other dancers closed off my view. . . . She had blonde hair and so I was wrong. But it shook me—and I wondered how there could be two girls in the world who had figures and legs like that. I patted the shoulder of another Barbary pirate and retrieved Suzie. She started to laugh as we swung away to a tango.

"You know who that was I was dancing with?" she asked.

"No. Who?"

"It was Vico!"

It was so funny that she had to stop dancing for the moment. I stood solemnly and watched her mirth, then moved toward her to resume our dance. There was a tap on my shoulder. I turned my head and looked into two black holes in a jeweled mask. Mlle. Swan Lake and her toreador were standing side by side looking at me. She said in English, "You've got Sleeping Beauty all awake now and laughing herself silly, so dance with me."

I grabbed the toreador's arm and pushed him toward Suzie. I said in Spanish, "Take over, chico," and I put my arm around Tita and got lost in the crowd.

"What the hell are you doing here?" I asked her.

She stopped dancing and pushed me away to look at me. Couples around remarked unpleasantly about our holding up traffic. She paid them no heed. She said, "That's the second time you've done that."

"Done what?"

"Asked me some insane question instead of kissing me."

I kissed her, and everything was all right with the world. Then we danced, very close and more or less in the same spot. I felt the joy of her and there was nothing in the universe except the two of us holding each other close and loving each other once more. . . . The music stopped. I led her to the alcove where Suzie and I had eaten our supper. I told her, "Never in my life have I been so happy to see anyone as I am to see you."

"You didn't recognize me," she said. "You looked right

132

at me, then you walked over to that—that whatever-her-name-is!"

"You know her name," I said. "It's Suzanne Lautrey. You've known her for years—just as Pete Dumbrowsky knew her for years and then finally fell in love with her. Why didn't you tell me about that, Tita?"

She shook her head and I went on.

"He had a date with her at the Hotel Nouvel and he was killed. You didn't know about that either, I suppose."

She shook her head again. "No, I didn't know, Alex."

I said, "I wish you didn't have that damned mask on. I want to see your eyes."

"To see if I am lying?"

"No, Tita, just to see them. I believe you. Let's not quarrel—not tonight. This is going to be a very special night, I think. Suddenly I knew everything I had to know about us, when I held you in my arms again."

"All right," she said. "I guess I'll take you back. . . . That Suzie!"

"Now will you tell me why you came here?"

"I've just told you—to see if I would take you back!"

"Is that what you told me? I guess I missed it. But why did you really come?"

"I love you enough to put up some fight! Do you think I'm a mouse? . . . And I solved Father's cryptogram."

"You solved what?"

"That Bank of Algiers note. I told you it was a message. It was based on the letter, of course. You had to have the banknote and the letter, and the rest was merely a matter of trial and error. Oh, I know all of his codes and his crypts and his methods. The number on the bill was AX-0837295. The "A", then is one and the "X" is twenty-four. So you take the first word and the twenty-fourth word in each paragraph and you write them all down, one after the other. This gives you twelve words because there are six paragraphs. Then you write the numbers 0-8-3-7-2-9-5 over each letter, repeating as you come to the end of the number, and to the end of the letters. You have a long string of letters and each has a number on top. The first number is zero, so you take that letter as is. The next number is eight, so you count eight letters away from the one you have

133

written, and that gives you the second letter. You repeat that all the way through and you have the message. It was a message in English, which Father spoke fluently. It said, (s.c.) 'MY OTHER HALF OF BROKEN PROMISE IS BARODI'. So I came here to see you. To see what you would do."

"Does Barodi know you are here?"

"I telephoned him Monday night and told him that Pedro and I wanted to come to the ball."

"Has he come down to the ballroom yet?"

"No. When he does, one of the orchestras will play his special music. That is an old custom."

"What music?"

"The andante movement of Tschaikovsky's Sixth. They play an arrangement of the theme. . . . I made the arrangement."

"You are a musician, too!"

"Oh yes. I have a lot of vices that you will have to find out about."

"Will you show me the way to Barodi's apartment, Tita?"

"It is forbidden to go there! He has it well guarded, Alex. You could not get near him."

"I know how," I said. "Tell me where it is."

"It's in the south wing, overlooking the Mediterranean. Come, I will point out the windows to you."

She led me to the other side of the ballroom, to an alcove where the windows looked out upon the *cour carré*. She drew the heavy curtains aside and she pointed to a row of windows on the top floor directly above the wide arched gate that led to the court. "All those windows on the top floor are his," she said. "The sitting room is in the center—those two windows. Then the dressing room and the bath. There are stairways from both the east and west wings and elevators on each side. But don't use the lifts—they make a lot of noise in the apartment and he doesn't like anyone in them but himself."

She turned her head towards me and I kissed her. I said, "Why did you put on a blonde wig, Tita?"

"Huh! Do you think I wanted to make it easy for you?"

"For me—or for someone else?"

She shivered then. "I know Vico is here," she said.

"If I don't see you before the unmasking, go down to the harbor. *Le Bouc* is tied up down there and Dohaine and Bernard are aboard. . . . Don't take off your mask here, Tita. Will you promise?"

She nodded. She said, "Find Pedro before you leave me, darling."

We went out on the dance floor and danced the last few bars of a rhumba. I spotted Pedro enmeshed with a semi-nude nymph and I tapped him on the shoulder as a fox-trot began. He relinquished his nymph and danced away with Tita, saying nothing. I looked at the nymph and she looked at me. She said, "Well, big boy, let's get to work. We're not going to press any grapes standing still."

So we pressed grapes—until another grape-presser came along.

I walked around the ballroom and looked over the Barbary pirates. I stood next to a couple of them and finally selected one that was very nearly my own size. I tapped him on the shoulder and said in his ear, "I have a message for you."

He looked startled, then said, "What?"

I motioned for him to follow me. I led him to an alcove nearby. The curtains had been drawn back and the windows were being used by couples as egress to the formal gardens on the east. I said, "The boss told me to tell you, Bodine went into the garden just now and he is to be watched."

"Bodine!" he said. "Has he been spotted already?"

"Certainly. I will point him out to you."

"Fine. Come on." He had his hand on the latch, then turned back to me.

"Who are you? Why are you dressed like that?"

"Never mind silly questions. I work for Starbruck, the same as you. Do you want me to show you Bodine or not?"

"Sure," he said. "Sure—I was just asking. They told me we'd all be dressed like pirates, that's all."

He opened the window and walked into the garden and I followed. "He went over that way," I said, pointing to a grove of trees to the left, just discernible in the moonlight.

135

We walked along flagstone walks and gravel paths, passing any number of couples locked in embraces. As we got to the more secluded part of the garden there were the sounds of male and female in the act of love. I made a show of peering at all of these, and my companion did likewise but with possibly a different motive. He stopped at the edge of the grove and said, "Jesus, I've got to get a dame! This drives me crazy! . . . Have you seen him?"

I'd taken the American .38 from the mink shoulder holster and I came up close to him. I said, "Not yet." Then I hit him hard on the back of the head with the gun. He grunted, then started to fold up. I caught him under the arms and dragged him into the grove along a narrow path. I moved slowly, fearing to encounter love-makers, but luck was with me. There was no one else in the grove.

I took off the guard's costume, working as quickly as I could in the dark. It was not easy. He was a big man and heavy to move around. He started to grunt and shake his head while I was taking off his pants. I hit him again, not gently. I finally got him stripped down to his underwear and I dragged him off the path and into a thicket. I hit him once more, on the temple, for luck, then took off my own costume and put on his. I pillowed his battered head on my ermine cape and draped the rest of Prince Charming over him, in case he wanted something to wear when he woke up. I adjusted my mask and hurried back to El Dorado and the *bal du printemps,* no longer a prince but a Barbary pirate.

18

I HURRIED THROUGH the garden to the ballroom and I spent ten minutes finding Pedro. He was back with his nymph and it wasn't easy to get him away. She had other ideas.

I told him, "Watch Martita. Don't let her out of your sight—and get rid of this nymph. You haven't got time for her tonight. I told Tita that I've got *le Bouc* down in the harbor. Bernard and Dohaine are aboard. Get Tita down there to the boat before the unmasking—that'll be around two o'clock. Don't let her take her mask off here. I'm depending on you, Pedro. Give me until three to get to the boat. If I don't show up by then, tell Dohaine to go back to St. Tropez. Don't wait for me."

He nodded his assent. He said, "I like your pirate costume better. . . . You were never a Prince Charming."

"Not to you," I said.

I stood on the sidelines for a moment and looked over the throng. Suzie wasn't in sight anywhere. A pirate passed by me and raised his right thumb in a surreptitious manner. I returned the salute and he nodded. Martita came around in the arms of a tall, thin Romeo. He was a good dancer and their feet were jiving to the rhythm of "St. Louis Blues," with a good trumpet to lead them. Pedro came up to them and tapped the Romeo. There was some discussion but Pedro was persistent.

I spent another ten minutes looking for Suzie. It wasn't that I wanted to see her; I just would have felt better to know where she was. And maybe, too, I was only wasting time and getting myself wound up to do what I was going to do.

I walked out the main doors of the ballroom and along the wide hallway to the large central hall which opened onto the courtyard. I passed a pirate at the main door who nodded to me and another scratching his buttocks in the empty hall, who ignored me. On my left was the corridor leading to the west wing, on my right that leading to the east. East or west? I picked on the east, which should have taken me to the main entrance to Barodi's apartment, the way Tita had described it. I strode purposefully and came to a turn to my right and a wide stairway. At the bottom leaning against the wall was a pirate. He looked at me and he said, "You are late." I said, "I know it," and I hurried up the stairs. There was another pirate at the top who said, "Wait a minute, monsieur. Where are you going?"

"Don't bother me," I said. "I'm in a hurry."

"Pardon, monsieur."

137

The stairway to the top floor was right in front of me and I ran up the steps to demonstrate my hurry. At the top a big pirate put up his hand and said, "No one is allowed on this floor, monsieur."

"I have an urgent message for the Count," I said. "Take me to his apartment."

He regarded me, unmoving. "What message? You cannot see the Count. He will not be disturbed."

"Oh yes he will! They've shot Bodine—out in the garden!"

"What! Shot him? Come with me."

He led me at a fast pace down the hall, then turned to the right and stopped before a great carved-oak door. I was surprised that there was no pirate standing guard there. He lifted a huge brass knocker and let it fall with a loud crack. The door was opened and another large pirate stood looking at us. He was not wearing a mask, like the others. He was a hard-looking hombre with a deep scar across his chin and his right ear well-cauliflowered. "Bodine has been shot," said the first pirate. "This man was sent to give the news to the Count."

The hard type backed inside and motioned for me to follow him. I stepped into a small windowless hall and faced another great door, but it wasn't made out of carved oak. It was of steel. The oaken door closed behind me and the pirate said, "I'll take your guns first, monsieur."

I handed him the pair in my sash. He put them in his own sash, where a single Luger was reposing, and turned to press a button high up at the side of the steel door. I unbottoned the third button of my black pirate shirt, reached in and took the American .38 out of the mink holster. When he was finished pressing the button and started to lower his hand, I hit him with the gun on the top of his head. I put a good deal of power into the blow.

He fell sideways as the door was opened. I stepped over him and pushed my way in, the gun in my hand. Another unmasked pirate inside was reaching for the gun in his sash when I cracked him on the side of the head. I caught him as he fell and tossed him outside with his unconscious companion. Then I closed the steel door and ascertained

138

that it was locked. I liked the idea of the steel door at my back.

I was in a small anteroom, completely mirrored, including the back of the steel door. I admired my rakish costume for a second, pushed one of the mirrors on this side, then on that until it swung open, and I was in a paneled hall with a door opening to the right and another straight ahead. The door to the right should have been to the kitchen. I opened the door ahead and walked carefully down a second paneled hall and to what I hoped would be the final door. I put my ear against it and listened. One man was talking—he seemed to be making a speech, but I could make out very few of his words. I checked the loads in my gun, swung the door open, and walked into the sitting room of the private apartment of the Count Sandor Barodi.

There was a large chandelier hanging from the center of the ceiling and this gave good light which etched clearly the faces of eight men sitting in a semi-circle in leather easy chairs and divans. All were dressed in costumes identical to mine and six of the eight wore masks, as I did. The two who were unmasked were both known to me. Occupying the central place in this group was a large oblong box on legs and in polished mahogany, not unlike a coffee table. There were regularly spaced grid-openings on the two sides I could see and a white electric cord ran from one end to a wall-plug in the right wall.

The man who had been speaking was silent. The room was as still as the death that pointed at them from my gun. I listened a moment and heard a slight whirring from the mahogany box. There is only one thing it could have been, a recording device so convenient for conferences in this electronic age.

"Sit perfectly still, gentlemen," I commanded. "Make no moves with your hands or your feet."

One of the masked men on my left started to move his hand to his waist. I shot him in the right arm. I got the shot off very fast, then moved the gun around to the others.

"Now, anyone else?"

All heads were turned towards me and there was no

more movement. The wounded man sat still, too, then suddenly slumped forward, his head on his knees.

"My name is Alexis Bodine," I said. "I came here to see only one of you. Now I see a second who interests me, whom I did not expect to find in this august gathering. Outside of these two, I have no concern or curiosity about your meeting or your identities. You are going to be permitted to leave. I want you to stand up, one by one as I point to you, drop your guns on the floor, then go over and face that wall. I warn you all, move carefully."

They did as they were.told, all except the wounded man. When they were lined up, I took this man's gun from him. Then I went to the mahogany box and opened the top. Inside was a big tape recorder, two reels spinning slowly. At each grid opening was a microphone. It looked like a very expensive apparatus. I clicked a switch marked *"Arrêt,"* then took off the reel on the right, upon which the tape had been winding. I broke the tape and put the reel in my sash at my back. Then I picked up all the guns from the floor and dumped them in a far corner. I approached the lineup of Barbary pirates. "Delacroix. Turn around and face me."

The *Sûreté* man, one of the two without a mask, turned and gave me his tired, old-world sneer. He drawled, "Hello, Bodine."

I said, "You've still got your police gun, a knife and a blackjack. Take them out very carefully and drop them on the floor. If you want to try a shot at me when you get your gun, go ahead. I'd just as soon kill you right here."

He nodded at me. "I know you would," he said. He took his gun out first, holding it with his fingers, and it thudded to the carpet. He took the knife from his sleeve and dropped that. The blackjack was in his sash and he tossed it to me. I caught it, hefted it, then put it next to the recording tape. "Sit down there and face me," I said, pointing to a divan.

"Vassily Bardov. You're next. Turn around."

The other unmasked man turned and faced me. He had a smooth, round face with a small button nose and a very few strands of blond hair left on the top of his head. But it was not a benign round face at all. The eyes were like

140

gray stones, hard and brittle, and the whole effect when he looked at you was of imperious, demanding, overpowering will. But only his face was hard—the rest of him was soft and rounded and as near voluptuous as a man can get.

"Vassily Bardov," I said, speaking softly. "It is very odd that I should remember you after all these years . . . I thought of you when I first heard of this Sandor Barodi business. But it didn't seem to make sense at all. Now it comes back to me—there were two of you. There was Bardov who was sometimes Barodi, and there was Barodi who was sometimes Bardov. Nobody cared much in those days—a name meant nothing and we were all working together in the *maquis* for the same purpose. So now that I see you again, I know there were two Barodis. Where's the other one, Vassily?"

He glared at me an instant, then twisted his mouth in a smile. "You killed him," he said. "You talked him to death, just as you are trying to do to me."

I said, "I see that you are still a very funny little man. Order your guests to depart—tell them to take their wounded companion with them. When they are gone, I will tell you and Delacroix what I want."

I stood behind the crescent of chairs and guarded the exodus. When they were gone, I told Bardov-Barodi to sit next to Delacroix and I sat facing them. I noticed that Barodi (I will call him that, to keep it simple) could not keep his eyes off the tape recorder.

"I turned it off," I said. "Also I took the tape."

He seemed to collapse, like a punctured tire. Delacroix exclaimed, "You can't do that! My God, man, you can't!"

I smiled at him. "It's done, and now, I would judge by your distress, that all of you will be done for."

Barodi had recovered his poise. He was going to play it cozy. He said, "There is nothing significant on that tape, only insofar as France and England are concerned. We are not occupied with the Americans. I will tell them all of my business any time they want to know it."

"Fine," I said. "I will remember your offer and pass it along to those who may be interested. . . . Meanwhile, of course, there are France and Great Britain, and your own

141

personal neck and Delacroix's, as well as the necks of your recent guests. Tell me, Count Barodi, was the Oran spice merchant Abdul-el-Krim among your guests tonight? Krim is a fine old Arab name. There was a Krim around Damascus in 1947 who was convicted of treasonable intercourse with the Russians, but a gang of his friends sprung him from the local lockup before he could be shot. Not the same man, of course?"

Barodi said, "You are wasting my time with all of this talk. I am a business man. How much do you want?"

"Three hundred and sixty million dollars," I said. "But not for the tape recording."

"You talk like an idiot, Bodine. Such a sum is fantastic! Where did you dream that up?"

"I'll tell you about that. First I want to know something else. Who killed Pete Dumbrowsky?"

He shrugged. It was an elaborate shrug. Maybe it wasn't too elaborate for the occasion. Maybe it was.

"I've got to have someone for that," I said. "How about Delacroix here? He'd make a good enough fall-guy."

Delacroix forgot himself and started to jump up. I waved the gun at him. "Easy," I said. "I told you I'm just aching to put a bullet in you."

"You son of a bitch," he said. He sat back down.

Barodi was laughing. "You want me to give you Delacroix! That is very funny!"

"Why is it funny?" I asked.

"I can't tell you," he said. "But it is!"

"I'm serious about this. I want you to tell me who killed Dumbrowsky."

"I know nothing about that. It was done against my orders."

"You know nothing about it but you know who did it."

He remained silent. Delacroix had gotten the old-world look back on his face and he was regarding Barodi.

I said, "You'll tell me before this night is over. We are going to do a lot of things you won't like. . . . We're going down to the port now and go aboard a boat. We're all going to review the past. There is only one way you can stay alive, Barodi, and that is to do what I tell you to do.

142

One of the things I'm going to tell you to do is to keep your promise to Don Carlos Ortega de Castro-y-Lomas."

He sat looking at me, his face expressionless. He was a hell of a poker player at that. Nobody in the world would have guessed he held nothing better than a four-flush.

I continued, "Martita de Castro will show you the letter that her father wrote to her and left for her in a safe deposit box twelve years ago. When you have read the letter, you will make your apologies to Mlle. de Castro and you will give her proper assurance that you will carry out the terms of the agreement stated therein."

"All right," he said after a long silence. "Tell me what I am to do."

"You will both go with me," I said. "You will put on your masks and we three will walk down the stairs together and to the *cour carré*. We will get into one of your cars and we will drive to the harbor. If there is a suspicion of a signal to anyone, by either of you, then I shall kill you . . . I don't think that I have to demonstrate further to you that I shoot very fast."

Barodi said, "No you don't. Shall I get up now?"

I nodded assent and I motioned Delacroix to his feet. I got two masks from a pile of them on a *directoire* table. When I handed the mask to Delacroix, I saw him measuring the distance between us and getting himself set. I said, "Don't try it."

We went out through Barodi's bedroom and down the stairway in the west wing. We passed three pirate-guards on the way down who saluted smartly—they knew Barodi all right—and another in the main hall who opened the door for us and ran to get a car at Barodi's order. We stood on the wide marble stairway waiting, Delacroix to my left, Barodi on my right, and myself a foot or so to the rear. The gun was in my hand. This wasn't a bluff. . . . The Sleeping Beauty in the pale green ballerina costume, with the be-jewelled bodice and the bright crown on her jet-black hair, came floating across the *cour-carré*. She carried a scarf in her right hand—it seemed to be wrapped around her hand as though it might have been hiding something she held there. I had heard the slam of a car door an instant before she appeared, and I assumed she had been in

143

one of the cars across the court. Wouldn't it be in such a manner that a young lady at a party such as this would take her needle of heroin? I had that thought, too. . . .

I watched her flashing legs in their net stockings and I had to admit to myself that she ran a very close second to Tita. Actually, she was much sexier in an earthy way—if you like your sex earthy. Both Delacroix and Barodi were watching her with concentrated interest. Barodi said, "I'd say that was Suzie except for the hair. I'll have to find out who she is."

Delacroix said nothing. She came to the foot of the steps and stopped, looking up at us. She said, "Three jolly pirates. I'll mow you down! Just try to board me!"

She waved the hand with the scarf in it and came slowly up the steps to our left. Barodi said, "That's Suzie's voice."

Delacroix leaned close to her when she was opposite him. He said, "Good evening, Suzie."

She stopped and faced him. Suddenly her left hand reached out and she snatched the mask from his face. She let out a blood-curdling scream. "You murderer! You killed him!"

Then her right hand came up, inches from his forehead, and there was a roar and a tongue of flame from the scarf. Delacroix fell at my feet as though he had been hit with a club. There was no top to his head.

Suzie ran screaming into the villa. I grabbed Barodi by the arm and pushed him down the steps. Our car was just coming up and I hustled him towards it. The pirate-doorman was running along side. The car braked to a halt and he opened the door. He asked, "What happened? I heard a shot?"

I pushed Barodi into the car and got in after him. I told the driver, "Go to the port, as fast as you can." The doorman slammed the door and we took off.

Barodi said, "My God, she shot him!"

"Right in the forehead," I said. "I had no idea it was going to come out that way!"

"She has been taking too much junk. Ever since Dumbrowsky died, she's been getting in deeper and deeper. And such a beautiful girl!"

144

"She just saved me a lot of trouble," I said. "I owe her something for that."

"It's going to cost a lot to fix this one," he replied. "They don't like you to kill *Sûreté* men."

"You can afford it," I replied.

19

I ARRIVED with Barodi on board *le Bouc* at two-ten. Martita and Pedro were not there, had not been seen. I told Dohaine to stand by on the bridge and shove off the minute they came aboard. I placed Bernard on guard with one of the machine guns—an old model Thompson .45 calibre —on the after-deck. I took Barodi to the cabin and told him to rest himself on the settee—that we were going to wait.

He had recovered a lot of his command and most of his acidity. He said, "You are an awful fool, Bodine, to think you can get away with this."

"I have gotten away with it, so far. The great Barodi kidnapped from his own impregnable fortress! . . . But I'm not very much interested in keeping you kidnapped, so don't get too comfortable. What I want to do is to put a bullet in you."

That silenced him for a few minutes. Then he said, "And the ransom, I take it, is this ridiculous agreement you say I made with de Castro?"

"Martita will show you the letter. It's up to her what she wants done about it. You do what she says. That way you will have a long and useful life."

"When my absence is discovered, they will find me and they will kill you. You've done this like an amateur! The driver who brought us here knows that we came aboard this boat. He will report it."

I said, "Sure he will. Then all they have to do is to find us."

I looked at my watch. Two twenty-five. I called Bernard

and he came into the cabin. I said, "Guard him. If he does anything you don't like, shoot him. If he starts to talk money, don't accept anything less than 360 millions in dollars. He's got that much to give away."

I went out on the *quai* and took a look around. *La Mouette* was tied up a hundred feet from us. Two men were standing in the stern looking my way. The *quai* was not well lighted and I could not see them clearly, but one had the size and the outline of Pateck. I hoped it was Pateck. I waved a hand at them, then turned toward the street that entered the port.

A taxi came rattling down the hill and turned into the *quai*. I ran toward it. Out came a toreador and a white ballerina with a feathered hat. The white ballerina ran up to me and threw her arms around me. The toreador stood and watched.

Tita said, "Police were all over the place. What did you do, steal the silver? We had to get out through the garden and climb down the mountain. We walked a mile before we found a taxi."

"Let's get aboard," I said. "We've been here too long already."

Dohaine had the engine going as we reached the side of the boat. Pedro helped Tita board and I cast off the lines. We were under way in less than a minute.

I took Tita into the cabin and I motioned Bernard outside. She said, "Uncle Sandor! What are you doing here?"

Barodi said, "Hello, my dear." His small stone eyes darted from her to me. He wasn't going to do the talking.

I said to her, "Show Uncle Sandor the letter from your father. I told him about it and he's dying to read it."

"Pedro has it," she said. "He's the only one with pockets."

I called for him and he came into the cabin. He gave Tita the letter and she handed it to Barodi. He read it slowly, scowling most of the way through it. Then he looked up at the three of us watching him and he laughed. I will credit him with a great deal of nerve. I would not have been able to conjure up a laugh at that juncture, under the circumstances.

146

"Who is this mysterious confidant of de Castro?" he asked.

"You," Tita said. "There was something else besides the letter and it named you."

"Pish and tush!" he said. "This has no more legal weight than a conversation in a boudoir! Just the ravings of a senile old man!"

"Senile!" exclaimed Tita. "You dare to say that?"

"Easy, honey," I said. "Don't argue with him." I hefted the .38, then I took a step to him and I slapped his face. It was a good, sound slap, not playful. I said, "Don't be stupid, these last few minutes of your life, Barodi. You're out in the Mediterranean without a friend in the world, drowning in your own evil juices. I am the only law here, and by God, your judge too! I decide everything—whether you live or you die!"

No fear showed on his face, but his voice shook when he spoke. He said simply, "What do you want?"

"Tita will tell you." I turned to her. "Tell him, darling. Tell him what you've decided will become of the money from the Spanish Treasury."

She was silent a long moment. Her hand reached for mine and I switched the gun to my left hand. Her fingers were ice cold. She said, "I don't want it for myself. I have plenty—Mother left me all of hers. I want it to go to the Sisters of Charity, as my Father planned."

"Do you hear that, Barodi?" I asked.

He nodded slowly. "I hear."

"Good. Then you will write out an authorization to Pedro Lomas to withdraw the full amount of these funds from the Swiss banks. Particularly Latrobe Frères. I have been told that you own Latrobe Frères. You will list the names of the banks and the account numbers. Pedro will fly to Switzerland tomorrow. He will notify me by telephone whether he has been able to obtain the funds. If he has been molested or hindered in any way because of incorrect authorization, you will die immediately. If he fails to call within a certain time, which I shall set, you will die immediately. If one little thing goes wrong, you will die. Do we understand each other, Barodi?"

147

"Yes."

"Pedro, get paper and a pen for the gentleman."

I removed all objects from the cabin that could be used as weapons and stored them in the galley. Then I locked the galley, put Pedro on guard with my gun, kissed Tita on the cheek, and went to the bridge. It was a beautiful spring night, with the sea as calm as a cast-iron horse. Dohaine, Bernard and I had a conference. *La Mouette* was about a hundred yards astern. Her running lights were out but there was enough moon to discern her outline.

"What course are you on?" I asked Dohaine.

"Zero six seven. We're going straight out into the Med."

"This is what we do. We capture *la Mouette* and we transfer those aboard to *le Bouc*. We tie them up securely and Dohaine takes them to Corsica. Propriano is a good place to get rid of them. Dohaine sends them ashore there. The bus service to Ajaccio is lousy and we won't be bothered with them for a couple of days. The rest of us—you Bernard, Tita, Pedro, and our guest Barodi—take *la Mouette* into Nice and we tie up at one of the *quais*. We send Pedro ashore and to Switzerland. If there's no regular flight out of the Nice airport in the morning, we'll charter a plane. Then we wait to hear from him, which should take only a few hours. If he is successful in his mission, I'll free Barodi and we'll scatter. If not, then we'll take Barodi back out to sea . . . I don't know about you, Dohaine. They'll be searching for your boat by air and sea. If they pick you up, you're going to be in a lot of trouble."

"I know Corsica," he said. "I can hide out there indefinitely. They'll never find me if I don't want them to."

"It should all blow over in a week unless I have to dispose of Barodi. Well, either way, it's not a very good prospect for you and Bernard. What do you think? We can abandon the whole thing right here and now and you'll be in the clear."

"No," said Dohaine. "We go through with it. I've come this far with you and I'll abandon nothing."

"I go too," said Bernard. "Only one thing—if we dispose of Barodi, I want to give him the last push."

"How about your job at the *sous-préfecture*?" I asked.

148

"I'll phone them from Nice," he said. "They'll think it's another woman. It won't be the first time. . . ."

Dohaine had three Tommy guns in a locker on the bridge. He gave me one and took one for himself. Then he slowed the engine. "We'll let them catch up," he said.

La Mouette came closer astern in about fifteen minutes, then swung out to our left and came even with us on our port side. I told Dohaine, "When the shooting dies down, swing your stern in close so we can board."

Bernard and I ran down to the afterdeck. La Mouette switched on a searchlight. It started to swing back to our stern from the bow and I shot it out with a short burst. A voice yelled an obscenity across the twenty-five feet of water separating the boats. I gave them another burst, high up on the cabin.

"Heave to!" I yelled.

There was an answering fusillade of pistol and rifle fire from la Mouette and one bullet whinged off a stanchion right next to my ear. Bernard and I both opened up in retaliation. We were both still shooting high.

"Heave to!" I yelled again.

Dohaine suddenly switched on his spotlight and it picked out two figures crouched low at the stern. One had a rifle aimed right at me. Bernard and I fired bursts together. The figure collapsed on the deck. The second man waved his arms frantically. "Cease fire!" he cried. "We give up!" He kept repeating, "We give up!" in a hysterical voice that finally cracked completely.

Dohaine came alongside the other boat and swung his stern in close. Bernard and I jumped aboard, our guns ready. The man who had been yelling had vanished. There was a body on the starboard deck near the rail. I went over and turned his face up. It was Pateck. I felt for a pulse. There was none.

"Cover me," I told Bernard. I went to the side of the cabin door and yelled in, "Come out one by one. Keep your hands in the air."

Four men came out and lined up on the deck. They were sullen but obedient. I pointed to Pateck with my gun. "The first two of you there, toss him overboard." The two indicated grabbed Pateck by the feet and shoulders and heaved him over the stern. Then they faced around, waiting for orders.

Dohaine was manoeuvring *le Bouc* close aboard. I told Bernard, "Get spring lines secured bow and stern. I'll guard them."

When the two boats were tied together Dohaine came down from his bridge and helped us. Bernard stood guard while Dohaine and I transferred the men one by one, tying up each with half-inch manilla. When all were secured I went to *le Bouc's* cabin and told Tita and Pedro what we had done. Barodi listened with expressionless eyes, the fingers of his right hand drumming on the cabin table.

"We now transfer to *la Mouette*," I said. I got some foul-weather gear out of a locker for Tita and Pedro and I helped her into the pants and jacket. Her ballet skirt bulged the oilskins to their fullest and she looked at them and laughed. "I guess I'd rather be warm than beautiful at that," she said.

I shooed her out of the cabin and I changed back into my St. Tropez suit. I took the reel from the tape recorder and I put it in my pants pocket. It was a tight fit, and as I struggled with it I saw Barodi eyeing me with avid interest.

"I'd give my life for that," he said.

"You'll give your life without it, Barodi."

He bowed his head. This exchange of boats seemed to have taken all the starch out of him. Whatever plan he was plotting or whatever hope had been raised for rescue was now ruined. He lowered himself on the starboard settee in *la Mouette's* cabin like a tired old man and sat back staring at the floor. I told him, "If there are any changes you want to make in those orders to the Swiss banks, you may make them now."

He shook his head, not looking at me. "Guard him close," I told Pedro. "We will come to the critical stage of our voyage very soon. If he attempts to cry out or in any other way attract attention, slug him. And don't be gentle about it."

I helped take our four captives into the cabin of *le Bouc* —it was too cold to leave them on deck—and Bernard and I double-checked their bindings. There was plenty of line

150

and we did each up like a trussed calf, then tied them all together.

I went up to the bridge, asked Dohaine the course to Nice, then we shook hands and bid each other adieu. "I'll expect to see you back in St. Tropez in about a week, if all goes well," I told him. "Otherwise you'll find me in some French prison—or graveyard."

"We used to talk about you in the War," he replied. "We used to say that if you could live through this operation, or that operation, then you were a bloody cat. So I'll be seeing you."

We found a berth at the *quai* docks in the narrow Nice harbor as dawn lighted the eastern sky. After tying up between a working-schooner that smelled like a garbage dump and a small tugboat, and giving a watchman a couple of thousand-franc notes, I went to the cabin. It was a much larger cabin than *le Bouc's* and there were settees port and starboard. Tita was asleep on the port side and Pedro sat at her feet, the gun in his hand and his eyes wide open. Barodi was sitting up on the other settee, leaning against pillows and his feet up on the cushion. His head was bent to his chest and he was snoring gently.

I told Pedro to get some sleep and I pointed forward. "There are three bunks in the crew's quarters," I said. "Get into one. I'll wake you."

He handed me the gun and left. I sat down at Tita's feet and watched her sleep. Then she opened her eyes and smiled at me. She said, "I'm getting used to you and your abrupt manner. I was just dreaming about telling people off, the way you do. . . . I bet we make the most disagreeable couple in all of Virginia."

We talked for a couple of hours while Barodi continued to snore. We made a lot of plans and we assumed that we would live forever and be together always—just as the very young do. At eight-thirty I awoke Pedro and Bernard, who had bedded down in an adjoining bunk. I gave Pedro most of the money I had left—nine ten-thousand-franc notes—and told him to buy clothes first, then get to Geneva by air. He had the five bank drafts, or orders, written and signed by Barodi and made out to himself. I told

151

him to go to Latrobe Fréres first. The bulk of the money would come from that bank. If there was no trouble there and he got the money, he was to go to the other banks in Geneva. When he had all of the funds from the Geneva banks, he was to deposit them in an account by number only, using no name, at Barclay, Waltham et Cie.

"Then telephone me at three p.m., no later, at the restaurant just across the *quai*—Chez les Pêcheurs. The telephone number is 69.61—you can see it on their sign hanging in front. I will be in the restaurant waiting for your call about a quarter to three and I will wait until about ten minutes after. If I do not hear from you, I will leave Nice with the boat. . . . Well, if I don't hear from you, it probably won't matter to you what I do or what becomes of all of us. I must warn you, Pedro, that this is an extremely perilous mission for you and that it may cost you your life. If you feel that you don't want—"

He stopped me with an upraised hand. "Enough of that kind of talk," he said, smiling. "It is not as dangerous as you say. In Switzerland one is under very competent police protection. I know that country well. . . . I will phone you no matter what happens. The police will permit a call, if worst comes to worst."

I liked his confidence. I needed some of it myself. I said, "Ask for M. Bernard, then. That is the name I will use in the restaurant."

He put an oilskin raincoat over his costume and I walked up to the deck with him. He jumped ashore, waved goodbye, and strode across the *quai* to seek a taxi.

I returned to the cabin. Tita gave me back my pistol. Barodi was awake. He had been talking to her and my entrance had stopped him in mid-sentence. I asked her in English, "What's new?"

"Lover boy was telling me what a vicious, murdering son of a bitch you are, darling. I told him I knew that. Then he said that if I would give him the gun he would kill you and set me free of you. Well, I was just about to give it to him when you came in and spoiled it all." Then she said in French, "I've been wondering if he puts a high enough value on his life to have written those bank orders properly

152

and in such a manner that they will be honored without question."

I looked at Barodi's round, grim face, the hard eyes glaring at me with hate, and I nodded my head. "Yes," I said, "I believe he does. Money does not come first with Barodi. It comes second."

The telephone call came through at three-five p.m. for M. Bernard at Chez les Pêcheurs. I took the receiver from the hands of the *patron*, who had answered the ring, and I listened to a strange voice say, "This is the police of Geneva, Switzerland, calling." My heart dropped to the pit of my stomach with a thud that shook me completely. I drew in my breath sharply and got ready to say something—anything—and the voice continued, "Just a moment, monsieur. There is a gentleman who wishes to speak with you."

Then Pedro's voice came on the phone. He spoke Spanish. He said, "Everything's fine."

"Thank God! What are you doing with the police?"

"I had to have a guard for all of that money. Do you think I want to take any chances?"

"Tell me what happened."

"Nothing. Latrobe Frères are my uncles—all five of them."

"Speak French. I can't follow you."

"The first deposits have been made at Barclay Waltham. The police are buying me beer. Can you imagine, with all of that money I have for beer! I'm leaving in a half hour for Zurich to get the rest of it. That's all to tell."

"I want to know what happened at Latrobe Frères."

"They paid off, that's all—oh yes, I nearly forgot! There was a friend of yours there, drawing out all of his money. He offered to buy me dinner. Vico del Oro!"

"These rats get off the ship quick," I said.

20

I FOUND A TAXI, a relatively recent Hotchkiss, outside Chez
les Pêcheurs and I told the driver to pull up on the
other side of the *quai*—opposite that boat there—and that
I would give him a very remunerative commission. He
showed practically no interest but he did as I requested
nevertheless.

I went aboard *la Mouette* and found our little company
in the cabin waiting for me. I addressed Tita first. I said,
"The Sisters of Charity are going to bless you for sure."

Then I turned to Barodi. "The three of us—Mlle. de Castro, M. Bernard, and myself—are now going to depart. We
will leave you alone here. You may do as you wish. You may
follow us to the *quai* and yell for the police. You may run
after the taxi I have waiting and point to us as kidnappers
and murderers. . . . Or you may wait here a decent inter-
val, then leave the boat and return with dignity to Villa
El Dorado. Just remember one thing, Barodi—I still have
the tape recording. I give you my word that no one shall
ever hear it, with the possible exception of Tita and myself in the event we get bored with good music and must
find a way to amuse ourselves of a dull evening in Virginia. There is one stipulation, however, and that is that
no harm of any sort, no matter how trivial, shall come to
Tita or M. Bernard or M. Dohaine—or any of my friends
here in France as a result of your efforts. And yes, that in-
cludes Mlle. Suzanne Lautrey, who must be absolved in the
slaying of Pierre Delacroix at any cost, and who must be
placed in a hospital or proper institution for cure of nar-
cotics addiction. That is the stipulation. As for myself, feel
free, Count Barodi, to make a try for me at any time. Either
you or your friends. I shall welcome them. Bernard, give
me my gun."

The three of us walked off *la Mouette* and got into the

taxi. We were not followed by Barodi. No outcry was raised. The police were not summoned.

"Go to Grasse with all haste," I told the driver.

"To Grasse, monsieur? The town of Grasse?"

"Yes. You go around the port and turn South and presently you will come to the *quai* des Etats-Unis, and you continue—"

"I know the way to Grasse," he interrupted.

Tita said, "I must say you are in a disagreeable humor. May I ask why we are going to Grasse?"

"You may. First we must deposit M. Bernard, who has put himself to great inconvenience on our behalf. Then we must inconvenience him further by having him arrange for our immediate marriage at the closest *mairie*. He knows everyone in Grasse and he can cut through all the red tape so that, I am certain, we may get married before sundown."

"I can't!" exclaimed Tita. "I have no clothes—I. . . . Listen! I won't do it!"

"See?" I said, "I knew that's the way you'd act when you got up to the barrier. That's why I'm in a disagreeable humor."

"But darling! We can't do it this way! I must have—I must have time! I must have my clothes!"

"So! You think you're going to procrastinate, eh? I will give you time and I will buy you suitable attire—in Grasse. The time you will have will be about fifty minutes, which should be ample for you and ample for this vehicle to take us to our destination."

"May I say something?" asked Bernard.

"Yes, go ahead."

"It is this, M. Janvier. Why are you always so pigheaded? Why don't you let Mlle. de Castro do it as she wishes?"

"Is that all you have to say?" I asked.

"No, it is not. I want to tell you also that you—"

"You leave him alone!" interrupted Tita. "If he wants to get married right away, it's his business, not yours. And he's not pigheaded. How dare you say he's pigheaded!"

"You see?" I said to Bernard. "You've got to learn to keep out of these family discussions. You just arrange for

155

the license and the mayor and I'll worry about the rest of it."

"Yes," said Tita. "That's all you've got to do."

The driver turned his head and said, "If this is a wedding party, may I offer my congratulations?"

"Thank you," said Tita.

The happy couple were married in the *mairie* at Grasse at five-thirty o'clock by M. Gaston Vannier, who had been Octobre in the Fox Group. The bride wore a beige suit by Balenciaga, which had been delivered from Nice after many frantic phone calls by Mme. Vannier, who operated the one good dress shop in the town. The bride wore a white feathered hat that looked suspiciously like the headdress from a stage costume. The maid of honor was Mlle. Lucienne Dohaine, who happened to be in Grasse visiting her aunt, and the best man was Aristide Bernard, who qualified for the duty by possessing a cutaway, striped pants, and an ascot. The witnesses included Sebastien Luchon, who, unfortunately, didn't have time to get out of his police sergeant's uniform and so made it appear that there was something sinister and, shall we say, "urgent" about the ceremony; Jules Simon, the ancient waiter from the Bianchi, who also wore a cutaway and ascot tie; Anton Gerber, who came over from St. Raphael to cash another American check; and last but not least Pépé from the Villa Le Trayas, who was in Grasse on business with the *sous-préfecture*—he had failed to renew his *carte d'identité*—and encountered the wedding party entering the *mairie*.

A reception followed at the home of M. and Mme. Vannier and a prodigious amount of champagne was consumed by the guests, most of them friends of the Vanniers, but all relatives or close friends of the former Fox Group members and so, by right of inheritance or association or what, friends of the happy couple.

The bride and groom managed to sneak away at seven-thirty o'clock in an automobile rented for the occasion from the local Citroën agency.

The bride said, "Well, now that you've had your way

156

about this silly business, let's go home to St. Raphael and go to bed. I'm tired."

What else is there to tell? Tita and I live in Eastmoreland, Virginia, but not too often. I've abandoned the banking business and Old Lawson—although I still hold the controlling shares in the bank. Also I have something else to do nights now other than play bridge—although on the few occasions we have played Tita has been very patient with me, and she has promised to teach me the finer points of Goren. . . . Oh, yes. Colonel Updyke.

I didn't keep my promise to him. I didn't tell him what I'd found out. I had it in the safe in my bedroom—the reel of recording tape. And I knew everything that was on it—the names, the dates, the events, and the treasons that were past and projected. But a bargain is a bargain, and I had made one that superseded any promise I'd made to him.

I met him in New York one day for lunch, at his request, and he said, "We've heard that you have something in your possession that could blow this whole mid-East thing apart."

"Where did you hear that?" I asked.

"It's a funny thing—it comes from a guy who's been working for us for years, and yet I personally have never trusted him. He's a Russian and once carried a lot of weight with the Kremlin crowd, then fell from grace, escaped from the country, and came over to our side. General Deschines was his only contact with Bu-X, and when the General died we were all left high and dry. Nobody knows who he is. We hear from him four or five times a year—always in one of our best codes and by registered mail to a postoffice box in Holland. The letters are usually mailed from some town on the Riviera—anywhere from Menton to St. Tropez. That's all we know. . . . Oh, we have a name, sure, but it doesn't mean a thing. These people change their names with their underwear."

"If you don't trust him," I said, "why bother? Obviously he's not to be trusted if he says I have anything of importance."

"You haven't, then?"

157

I shook my head. "Nothing that you should see or hear or get in a swivet about. . . . Sure I picked up some stuff when I was chasing Delacroix and Barodi, but you don't need it."

He sat pulling on a pipe and looking into his empty coffee cup, thinking his thoughts. Then he said, "It's funny that you should use the word 'hear'. I didn't tell you what it was you were supposed to have."

"No you didn't. What is it?"

"A tape recording. One hour and a half of a meeting among the eight men who pull all the wires in the mid-East and North Africa."

It was my turn to do some thinking. I lit a cigarette and I thought. I said, "What's the name of this man—the name you have?"

He said, "I shouldn't give it to you. It's one of the tightest secrets we've got in the bureau. . . . Well, the hell with it. You're involved, just as much as though you were still working with us. The name we have is Vassily Bardov."

I looked blank, then shrugged. "As you say," I remarked, "these people change their names with their underwear . . . probably."